*Sweetheart, California's Something Borrowed provides celebrity weddings with bridesmaids and groomsmen for hire ... but once in a while what's purely business becomes the best kind of personal.*

**RULE #3: DON'T MIX BUSINESS WITH MIXED DRINKS**

Kelly Barrow, the founder of Something Borrowed, didn't get the happily ever after she counted on, but she considers herself fortunate anyway. After all, she has a thriving business and a loving family and friends. Yet ten years after her heartbreak, surrounded by couples in love, she knows it's time to move on—and the gorgeous actor who hires her for his sister's wedding seems like the perfect opportunity. There's just one problem. Her best friend and legal counsel, Christian Ryan, keeps getting in her way ...

Chris has been a shoulder to lean on since they were kids, and Kelly never expected him to interfere in her dating life. She doesn't realize that over the years, Chris's feelings have grown beyond friendship. The timing just never seemed right—until now. And as the two of them work through the wedding's inevitable surprises and disasters, Kelly begins to wonder if she's been looking for love in the exact wrong place ...

Visit us at www.kensingtonbooks.com

# Praise for Codi Gary's Something Borrowed Series

### Kiss Me, Sweetheart

"Winning…A delightfully romantic read."
—*RT Book Reviews*, **4.5 Stars Top Pick**

### Don't Call Me Sweetheart

"*Don't Call Me Sweetheart* is packed with laugh-out loud moments balanced by emotion that rings true."
—*RT Book Reviews*, **4.5 Stars Top Pick**

"Gary's novel will delight romance lovers who appreciate a strong heroine going after what she wants."
—*Publishers Weekly*

"Flirty, fun, and fabulous!"
—**Bestselling author Candis Terry**

"Fun, lighthearted, and full of emotion. You can't help but smile while reading Codi Gary."
—**K.M. Jackson, author of** *Insert Groom Here*

"Codi Gary is the queen of romance. She'll make you fall head over heels."
—**T.J. Kline, author of the Healing Harts series**

"*Don't Call Me Sweetheart* is a charming romance that will leave you saying 'I do, I do' to author Codi Gary."
—**Leah Marie Brown, author of the It Girls Series**

# Books by Codi Gary

The Something Borrowed Series
*Don't Call Me Sweetheart*
*Kiss Me, Sweetheart*
*Be Mine, Sweetheart*

The Rock Canyon, Idaho Series
*The Trouble with Sexy*
*Things Good Girls Don't Do*
*Good Girls Don't Date Rock Stars*
*Bad Girls Don't Marry Marines*
*Return of the Bad Girl*
*Bad for Me*
*Good Girls Don't Kiss and Tell*
*Good at Being Bad*

The Loco, Texas Series
*Crazy for You*
*Make Me Crazy*
*I Want Crazy*

The Men in Uniform Series
*I Need a Hero*
*One Lucky Hero*
*Hero of Mine*
*Holding Out for a Hero*

The Standalones
*How to Be a Heartbreaker*

Bear Mountain Rescue
*Hot Winter Nights*
*Sexy Summer Flings*

Lyrical Press books are published by
Kensington Publishing Corp. 119 West 40th Street New York, NY 10018

Copyright © 2018 by Codi Gary

All rights reserved. No part of this book may be reproduced in any form or by any means without the prior written consent of the Publisher, excepting brief quotes used in reviews.

All Kensington titles, imprints, and distributed lines are available at special quantity discounts for bulk purchases for sales promotion, premiums, fund-raising, and educational or institutional use.

To the extent that the image or images on the cover of this book depict a person or persons, such person or persons are merely models, and are not intended to portray any character or characters featured in the book.

Special book excerpts or customized printings can also be created to fit specific needs. For details, write or phone the office of the Kensington Special Sales Manager:
Kensington Publishing Corp.
119 West 40th Street
New York, NY 10018
Attn. Special Sales Department. Phone: 1-800-221-2647.

Kensington and the K logo Reg. U.S. Pat. & TM Off.
LYRICAL PRESS Reg. U.S. Pat. & TM Off.
Lyrical Press and the L logo are trademarks of Kensington Publishing Corp.

First Electronic Edition: August 2018
eISBN-13: 978-1-5161-0233-4
eISBN-10: 11-5161-0233-9

First Print Edition: August 2018
ISBN-13: 978-1-5161-0234-1
ISBN-10: 11-5161-0234-7

Printed in the United States of America

# Be Mine, Sweetheart

*Something Borrowed*

## Codi Gary

**LYRICAL SHINE**
Kensington Publishing Corp.
www.kensingtonbooks.com

*This book is dedicated to the amazing women and men who serve in our military. They spend months away from their homes and families, bravely putting their lives on the line. If no one has told you today, thank you.*

# Chapter 1

Kelly Barrow stared down at the court papers on her mahogany desk, completely flabbergasted. Her company and personal attorney, Christian Ryan, sat across from her in one of the black leather guest chairs. It was Monday morning in mid-May, and Kelly was tempted to open the blinds on her two office windows and let the sun in. Maybe it would shine a new light onto the terrible words mocking her from the white sheets of paper.

When she looked up at him, she could tell he was fighting a grin.

"This is a joke, right?" she asked.

Chris shook his head. "No joke. I received them this morning."

"Who in the hell sues someone for"—she read the amount again, and scoffed—"thirty-two dollars and seventeen cents?"

"Apparently, Wesley James, who didn't appreciate you walking out on a date with him."

"I didn't walk out! I told him that I had a work emergency and had to go!"

Chris shrugged his broad shoulders. "Guess he didn't believe you because he is suing you for the cost of your dinner and your ticket to… *Pirates of the Caribbean*."

This was one of the reasons why she hadn't dated in eleven years. Men were absolute idiots.

"Can you just take care of this? Send him a check or whatever so he will go away."

"Not that simple, Kel," Chris said. "The man wants a formal apology and for you to be his date for his sister's wedding."

Kelly looked down at the papers again and sure enough, that was what it said.

In bold print.

"Why would he want me to be his date if I pissed him off so bad he had to file a lawsuit against me?"

Chris shrugged. "The guy must be hard up. I can't think of a single reason he'd want to take you...oh wait." He ticked off his fingers as he spoke. "There's the fact that you're beautiful, intelligent, and will no doubt make whatever ex-girlfriend he's afraid of bumping into insanely jealous."

Kelly stuck her tongue out at him, but he just laughed at her childishness. She'd known Chris since eighth grade, when he'd walked up to her for his friend, Ray Jackson and told her Ray liked her. Chris had approached the subject with a smooth, charming air that he'd carried over into adulthood. It was part of the reason he made such an amazing lawyer.

She'd been floored at first and told him that if his friend wanted to talk to her, he should do it himself. She'd topped off that set down with a toss of her ponytail before spinning on her heels and heading for math class.

Later that day, on the way to the buses, Ray had finally approached her, with Chris in tow. The two of them had been opposites in appearance. Ray hadn't hit his growth spurt yet and was five feet eight inches, with dark skin and obsidian eyes. He had wide shoulders that cut into a V to his waist, well-muscled even at fourteen. His hair was shaved close to his head and his smile was wide and engaging, with a hint of shyness she'd been drawn to.

Chris had been tall and gangly. His long hair reached his shoulders and was pale yellow with streaks of gold. Light blue eyes were hidden behind Buddy Holly frames, and perched atop a slim nose. His full lips had been quirked into a smirk as he stood behind Ray, his hands in his jean pockets.

Ray asked if she wanted to grab some ice cream with them at the Sweetheart Creamery and she'd said sure. Although the walk to the ice cream shop had been a bit awkward, Ray had told a corny joke about cats. It broke the ice and she'd laughed. They'd gone inside, swapping spoonsful of ice cream and teacher horror stories. They'd left the creamery and while Chris had gone into the gas station to get them all slushies, Ray had slipped his hand into hers. She still remembered the warmth, the butterflies in that first experience. It was something that could never be duplicated.

After that moment, it had been the three of them together; Ray and her as a couple and Chris as their dear friend.

Then high school had ended, and Chris had gone away to college while Ray had joined the military. Kelly had gotten a job at the local bridal boutique and stayed right there in Sweetheart, California. She'd missed them dreadfully, and when Ray had come home on his first leave and asked her to marry him, she'd said yes. They'd started making plans for when his four years were up. She was already taking courses at Consumes River College in business, and when Ray got out, he would get his degree, too. They'd get jobs, get married, and eventually have four kids. The plan was to be happy and in love forever.

Only Ray had never come home. He'd been killed in action just before his twenty-second birthday, and Kelly had been a mess. Her parents. Her friends. No one could bring her out of her misery.

Until Chris had come back to town and sat on the bed next to her prone form. At first, he'd been patient and understanding. Bringing her favorite movies and treats, trying to get her to talk to him. When she still wouldn't acknowledge him though, he'd lost his temper. He'd grabbed her by the shoulders and turned her around to face him.

*"You aren't the only one who loved Ray, and he wouldn't want you behaving like this. You're so wrapped up in your own grief that you don't give a shit about anyone else who may be hurting."*

She'd come out of her depression enough to slap him, and the rush of emotions that followed had her pummeling his chest, screaming and cursing at him. Chris had wrapped his arms around her, holding her tight until she stopped fighting. When the dam broke, she just wailed. Sobbing her heartbreak all the while he cried into the crook of her neck. It had been Chris's tears that had been the key to fully waking her up. They'd held each other close as their grief had spilled out, Ray's death binding them in their mutual loss.

After Ray's funeral, Chris had gone back to Stanford, but they'd stayed close. It had actually been Chris who had told her that her idea of starting a bridesmaid-for-hire company wasn't such a bad one. They'd spend hours on the phone drafting her business plan together, laughing and arguing. She'd gotten her loan because of him.

When he'd finished law school, she'd begged him to come back.

And now, here they were, still friends. Poring over a frivolous lawsuit ten years later.

Kelly shot Chris a pleading look. "I don't really have to go out with him again, do I?"

Chris laughed, throwing back his head, and Kelly studied him. At thirteen, Chris had been a towheaded kid, beanpole thin with glasses. As a man, his white-blond hair had darkened to a rich gold, and he wore contacts over his light blue eyes. Kelly wasn't oblivious to the fact that Chris had become a handsome guy; it just didn't matter. He would always be Chris. Ray's best friend, and then hers.

"No, Kelly. I'll handle it."

She winked at him. "Thanks, C. What would I do without you?"

"Continue to date losers?"

"Ha ha," she said. "So funny."

"What did prompt you to go out with this guy?" Chris asked. "He must have had some game."

Kelly shifted in her chair awkwardly, embarrassed to tell him that she had joined an online dating site, but she didn't lie to Chris.

"I wouldn't really say that. I signed up on LastFirstKiss.com and that guy was one of the top matches the website spit out."

Chris arched one of his golden eyebrows and pointed to the complaint on her desk. "Seriously? *This* guy is the best online dating has to offer?"

"Apparently. When he contacted me, and I saw his profile, it all looked good. He had a steady job, he was attractive…"

She trailed off, and he waved he hand for her to go on. "So, what happened?"

She grimaced. "He lied on his profile."

"Shocker," he deadpanned. "What did he say? That he was six two instead of five two?"

Kelly scowled at him. "I'm sorry, I'm looking for Chris? My fantastic, supportive best friend?"

Chris shot her a sheepish grin. "Apologies. Your S.B.F. is back."

Kelly hesitated for a moment, studying his face to make sure he was done being a punk. When she was satisfied he would keep his sarcasm to himself, she continued.

"He lied about everything, including what he liked to do for fun! At dinner, I asked him where he liked to go dancing and he said he only put that on there because *girls* liked that! I could have let that go, but he was a complete douchenozzle to the waiter at the restaurant. The kid took our order, and came by to let us know that the kitchen was backed up. All he did was ask if we wanted a complimentary appetizer while we waited, and Wesley went *off*. I was so embarrassed and would have taken off right after that, but he left the waiter a note of apology and a nice tip, so I thought, fine. Maybe he just had a bad reaction to low blood sugar."

"I take it that wasn't the case?" Chris asked.

"Nope. We got to the movie and he didn't even ask what I wanted to see, just told me he'd bought the tickets online ahead of time. I pointed out that I might have already seen the movie he picked and basically, it didn't matter because it was the only thing *he* wanted to see. I was grinding my teeth by this point. The final straw though was when he put salt on the popcorn I bought after I told him *I* didn't like salt on my popcorn."

"How'd he do that? Didn't you have control of the container?"

"I did, until I asked him to hold it while I went to the little girls' room. We sat down in the theater, I took one bite and almost ralphed."

"What'd he say when you called him out on it?" he asked.

"I didn't. I handed it to him and asked if he wanted it because I wasn't hungry anymore. Frankly, after that, I was relieved when Veronica called me and pulled me out of the movie. The way he chewed popcorn was just…disgusting. Plus, between his selfish tendencies and mood swings, I was a little freaked."

Chris chuckled. "Ah, Kel, I love you."

"I know."

They shared a smile over the desk. Since the first time they'd watched a *Star Wars* marathon in high school, Chris and she had done the Han Solo and Princess Leia bit. It used to drive Ray crazy, not because he was jealous, but because he hated *Star Wars*. That had never stopped them, though.

"Speaking of business, have you talked to Dustin Kent about his brother's estimate for restoring Buzzard Gulch? It seems kind of high, don't you think?" Chris asked.

Buzzard Gulch was her friend and former employee, Marley Stevenson's baby. She'd convinced Kelly that they could turn the old ghost town into a premier wedding venue. They'd brought Dustin Kent into the project because he held the deed to the land and was one of the biggest investors. Rylie Templeton had a stake in the deal, because Marley had convinced Kelly that having company bakers, florists, and other wedding vendors would bring in more revenue. Rylie had been an asset as a bridesmaid and now, as the exclusive wedding cake maker, was essential to Something Borrowed's future.

"I'm going to talk to him, but honestly, I think he's being generous with us. Building materials and permits are not cheap."

Chris sat forward in his chair, a solemn expression on his face. "Still, I don't want you getting in too deep. Especially if you're going to find a trophy husband; you gotta be able to make it rain."

"Shut up." At his grin, Kelly leaned her head back in the chair and groaned. "Ugh, I don't know what to do. I haven't been dating since LFO was cool and it was only ever with one guy. I don't know how to do this."

"Then don't. No one says you have to date."

No one had to say it. Her own mind had been demanding it for almost a year, but even before that, it had been a struggle. For eleven years, she'd created beautiful, perfect memories for brides and grooms. The first few had been the most painful, always imagining what it would have looked like on Ray's and her wedding day. After about five years, the pain had lessened, replaced by the ever-growing jealousy of others' good fortune. She still loved what she did, but there was an envy to it now. Kelly had even created a secret Pinterest page with ideas for her own special day, when or if she ever had one.

Still, it had seemed too soon, and when she'd never developed feelings for anyone else organically, she'd finally decided to take her romantic life into her own hands.

Would Chris understand? Ray had been his best friend, but he didn't expect her to never find love again, right?

She met his gaze sadly, but determined to be strong. "It's time. I used to think that my future died with Ray, but the truth is, watching all my friends find love and get married, start families… it made me realize I still want those things. I'm thirty-one years old; I need to move on."

Chris didn't say anything for several moments and she sat forward. "Don't you think?"

She couldn't tell what he was really thinking, but when he nodded, she almost sighed aloud in relief. She couldn't have Chris disappointed in her. He was the most important person in her life.

Chris reached across the desk, taking her hand in his.

"You deserve to be happy, Kel. I'll support you in whatever you do. You know that."

Kelly squeezed his hand back. "Thanks, Chris. What would I do without you?"

# Chapter 2

Chris was an unsupportive dick.

Okay, maybe not out loud. But for the last three days in his head, he hadn't been able to shake the urge to call Kelly up and tell her not to date. That dating was a stupid idea.

He hadn't because he couldn't come up with a single reason *why* she shouldn't.

At least none worth really considering, since he was currently out on a date himself. More than a date, really. He'd been seeing Cassidy Palos for over a year, and she was great. Funny, sweet, and pretty without being high maintenance. She was busy with her surgical residency, so she wasn't demanding, and they got along well together. He could see himself proposing in the future.

Yet the thought of Kelly finally getting back in the saddle and dating again had thrown him for a loop. In fact, he couldn't concentrate on what Cass was saying over the constant replay of Kelly's announcement in his head.

It wasn't that he wanted Kelly for himself. They were just friends, always had been. Of course, there had been times over the years where the thought crossed his mind that there could be more between them, but he couldn't bring himself to take that step with her. Kelly was too important and if they didn't work out, their friendship would be forever altered.

It dawned on him that Cass was frowning at him, annoyance flashing in her brown eyes. They were seating across from each other in the middle of the crowded restaurant. In the center of the table was a large candle, an empty bread basket, and a glass bottle of an oil and vinegar mixture. Their dinner dishes were stacked to the right, and they were just waiting on the waiter to come back with dessert.

"Chris? Did you hear a word I've said?"

*Not a one. Shit.* He hoped his smile was charmingly sheepish. "Sorry, I guess I'm tired tonight."

Cassidy's expression darkened, and he realized that she was *pissed*. It was strange because he'd never seen her truly angry before. They'd had little arguments, but never fought.

And he would have remembered that death stare.

"Really? *You're* tired?" she said snidely.

Okay, that surprised him. What the hell had he missed? "Uh, yeah."

"I have been up for forty-eight hours straight, performing numerous surgeries. Yet I still manage to listen to you drone on and on about whatever issue *Kelly* has with her wedding shop this week."

The way she dragged out Kelly's name rankled him. He'd introduced the two of them not long after Cassidy and he had started dating and they'd always seemed to get along. Not a whiff of jealousy or trouble between the two, so where was this animosity coming from?

"What is your problem tonight?" he asked.

She set her purse on the table and started rummaging through it, making the candle flame flick and weave. "My problem is us, Chris. When we started dating, you were the one thing I looked forward to. We'd go out, have fun, talk, make love…things were great. But it seems lately, I actually have to force myself to drum up the enthusiasm to get dressed for our dates."

Well, that was a blow to the good old ego. "Okay." He paused, trying to come up with a clever retort, but was too stunned by her frankness. "I don't know how I'm supposed to respond to that."

She rolled her eyes at him with a huff. "I'm bored, Chris. You're bored too, if you'd only admit it to yourself. You should be upset by what I'm saying, but you're not, are you? Because you're just as uninterested in my life as I am in yours."

Chris was floored to say the least. He wasn't uninterested in Cass, was he? Okay, there were times when his mind drifted a bit, especially when she started talking about bowel reconstruction, but that's just because the visuals it created made him queasy. There was a reason he chose a profession that did not have to contend with people's bodily functions and juices.

"Are you going to say *anything*?" she asked.

How had he never seen this side of her before? This angry, frustrated person who had obviously been bottling things inside. "What can I say? You've obviously made up your mind that it's over."

"No, I'm just saying it out loud. It's been over for months." She pulled out several bills and left them on the table. "I'm sorry if this is coming across as harsh. It's not that I haven't had fun with you, and I do like you as a person."

Chris held up his hand. "No need to try and make me feel better with whatever the *but* was attached to that sentence. I'm fine, really."

Cass sighed. "I know. That's what sucks. Because if you cared, you'd be fighting this right now."

Chris was pretty sure he wouldn't. If someone didn't want him, there was no way he was going to get down on his knees and try to change her mind. The only thing *that* did was make the dumper stay with the dumpee out of guilt and how was that fair to anyone?

Cass stood up, smoothing her hands over her navy dress. "Good-bye, Chris."

"You don't want to at least wait for the dessert you ordered?" he asked.

"No. I told the waiter on the way to the bathroom earlier to pack it up to go."

*Damn. I was looking forward to trying the Oreo cheesecake she ordered.*

"All right then. Have a good life."

She turned away without saying anything in return, and walked past the tables of happy couples talking over glasses of wine and low light candles. The hostess by the door handed a paper to go bag to her, and then she disappeared out the darkened door. A few of the women glanced at her walking out on him, and gave him concerned looks.

It was humiliating to be left alone in a romantic, dimly lit restaurant before the check came, but Chris was surprisingly relieved. Obviously, Cass had concluded their courtship had run its course first, but she was right. He'd gotten comfortable with their relationship, but ultimately, he hadn't been excited to go out with Cass. It had started to feel like a routine. If he'd been really paying attention, he would have realized that they hadn't had sex in nearly a month.

How in the hell had he not noticed *that*?

The waiter came by his table. He was a tall, gangly guy with a patch of hair on his chin. Chris hated the pitying expression in his gaze, so Chris grinned conspiratorially.

"Hey, do you mind adding two more slices of cheesecake to the bill? I'm heading to a *friend's* place."

The waiter's eyes widened for a second before he grinned. "You got it."

Now that his waiter thought he was *the man*, he could leave the place with some dignity.

He pulled out his phone and scrolled through the numbers, pausing on Kelly's name. It was a little past eight, and Kelly was a night owl. Dollars to donuts she was up binge-watching something.

Chris tapped on her name and shot her a text.

*You up for some company?*

*What happened to your date with Cassidy?*

*She dumped me before dessert.*

*Ouch. That sucks. But yeah, okay, you can come over.*

*I'll be there in forty with Oreo cheesecake.*

*Aw, are we going to have girl talk and eat our feelings?*

*Shut up.*

*Hey, I am letting you horn in on my Reign marathon. You better be nice to me.*

Chris laughed aloud, and after he paid for his meal, he walked to his car still grinning. One of the perks of having a friend like Kelly; unless she had a work emergency, she was never too busy to hang.

He lost his smile as he realized that was going to change once she started dating. And he was a jerk because he didn't want it to.

When they were teenagers, it had been Ray, Kelly, and Chris against the world. Sure, he'd gone off to school and Ray had been overseas, but they had kept in touch. Phone calls. Letters. Emails. They were still the three musketeers.

Until the day Ray died. Chris could still feel the raw pain in his chest when Ray's mom had called to give him the news. His thoughts had immediately gone to Kelly, of being with her and then they'd have each other to get through it. Chris had taken off in the middle of the night to get back to Sweetheart, and shown up at his parents' place at two a.m. It had been too late to go straight to Kelly's, but as soon as nine in the morning rolled around, he was knocking at her front door. After Chris managed to snap her out of the grief-filled haze she was in, things were immediately better being near Kelly. It was as though a little part of Ray was still with them when they were together.

He'd stayed for as long as he could, but it still hadn't felt long enough. Kelly had come to visit him a couple times, but once she got Something Borrowed up and running, she hadn't been able to get away as much.

On his breaks, he'd come home, eat dinner with his parents, and then take off to visit Kelly. He'd moved back after law school to be close to her. And over the years, no matter what was going on or who he was dating, Kelly was always there.

About a year after Ray had died, he'd waited for Kelly to start dating again, but it never happened. The one time a friend had tried to set her up, she'd called him because she was sick to her stomach. He'd come up for the weekend with ginger ale and a couple movies, and she'd blown off the date. He hadn't heard her talk about it since. Did she ogle actors in her favorite movies and television shows? Absolutely, but he hadn't heard her talk about a real man. Not until those papers had shown up, suing her for a lousy date. It was almost comical that anyone could have a bad time with Kelly. She was amazing.

And despite working together and spending most of their free time together, they'd managed to stay friends.

Now, she was going to meet someone and what if it wasn't like with Ray? What if the new guy was jealous of their friendship? If the guy didn't get their *Star Wars* jokes or their obsession with Korean television dramas? Not that he'd ever admit to Kelly that he liked the shows she forced him to watch, but all of that would be gone if she got serious with someone.

Chris shook his head at the direction of his thoughts. He really did sound like a complete, selfish asshole. Kelly was his friend and she deserved to be happy. Just because she was dating, didn't mean that things had to change for them.

And even if it did, he would still be there for her. They had been through too much to drift apart because of some faceless guy.

*A faceless guy who's going to do everything I've been doing for her, but he'll be getting perks.*

Chris jumped as the thought came unbidden. Perks? With Kelly?

No, he didn't want that. And he didn't care if she called the future guy to fix her door, or grab her donuts or come over to kill a spider.

Chris was completely fine with it.

# Chapter 3

The next day at work, Kelly sat at her computer and scrolled through the emails she'd gotten overnight on TheLastFirstKiss.com. There were fifteen in total, and the first four she'd already slipped into the trash bin on principle. Men who started off emails with *Baby, you are so hot* or *damn, you got a nice frame* did not even warrant a response. She clicked on number five, sent from a guy with the username FishGuy79, and smiled.

*Hey WeddingGrl31. I promise, if you let me take you out, I will not bore you once. Okay, maybe once, but if you snore, I won't hold it against you.*

This guy was funny, which held promise. She hopped over to his profile and...

Good God, *that* was a long ass beard. Like *Duck Dynasty* on Rogaine long.

Kelly tilted her head to the side, considering if he shaved it, he might not be so bad.

She'd put him in the maybe pile. She could handle a guy with a beard if he kept it trim. And the flannel lumberjack look *could* be sexy.

When she clicked onto the next email for OneFineEvoDude she smiled. He sounded intelligent. At least he could form full sentences with proper grammar and punctuation. Several emails had been nothing but short hand, and it had been hard to decipher what some of the abbreviations meant.

She wrinkled her nose when she clicked on his name and saw his picture. Kelly couldn't even say whether he was attractive or not. She was too distracted by everything else. He was wearing a neon yellow tank top and sporting a man bun next to his powder-blue Prius.

Nope. Beards she could handle, but hipsters with man buns were out.

Kelly sank back into her chair with a sigh, completely deflated. It was Friday morning, and tonight most single people would be getting ready for their dates. Yet she'd scrolled through what seemed like hundreds of profiles and there was not one that sparked anything in her. No interest. Not even a flick of curiosity.

She stood up and ran her hand along her bookshelf. It was filled with bridal magazines, wedding planning books, and a handful of romance novels mixed in for her down time that Rylie had told her she *had* to read. Across her office on the red, textured wall were framed accomplishments. Her wedding for actress Mia Ryder splashed across the cover of *People*. A framed copy of her first commission check. A "Thank You" letter from Governor Marcus Barker after she had managed to arrange for his son to parachute in for his own wedding while on leave from the military.

None of these things filled the lonely space in her heart that wanted a man of her own.

Someone knocked on her office door, and she ran around the back of her desk, skidding in her stocking feet on the wood floor. She caught herself on the desk and closed the screen quickly. She did not need any of her employees seeing what she'd been searching. The only person she'd told about TheLastFirstKiss.com was Chris.

"Come in!"

Veronica Torres poked her head in, her dark hair hanging in loose waves. "Hey, boss, there is a weird guy here saying you have an appointment."

"Weird how?" Kelly knew she had an appointment with actor Hank Townsend regarding his little sister's wedding, but Hank wasn't what she'd consider weird. Hot. Panty-melting, definitely. He had to be to land some of the highest-paying roles in Hollywood. Women didn't watch action flicks because they enjoyed planes blowing up and elaborate car chases. At least, *she* didn't. And she had every movie he'd ever made on her shelf.

Yeah, she might have been a *wee* bit obsessed with him and trying hard to hold her inner fan-girl at bay.

Veronica lowered her voice to a stage whisper, her red lips twisted in disapproval. "He's wearing one of those stupid fake glasses and nose things and he's talking in a really bizarre accent."

"I can hear you, you know," a deep, Scottish brogue said dryly from out of sight.

Veronica shrugged. "I know."

Kelly smothered her laughter with a cough. Hank was big on being incognito, but sometimes his disguises caused more of a stir than if he'd just been himself. The tabloids loved to paint him as eccentric and strange, so it was no wonder Veronica thought so as well.

Plus, Veronica had a low bullshit tolerance. It was the only reason Kelly hadn't promoted her to wedding expert yet. Dealing with stressed out brides was a high-pressure gig. There was a lot of biting your tongue and smiling, and Kelly just wasn't sure she could placate.

"Let him in, Veronica."

"Okay." Veronica pushed the door wide and addressed someone out of sight. "You can come on in, sir."

Kelly stood. When Hank walked into the room, Kelly had to bite her lip to keep the giggles at bay. Hank was wearing a loud, red Hawaiian shirt that did nothing to hide his broad, muscular shoulders. A straw hat sat cockeyed on his full head of dark hair, and his glasses and nose even had a black plastic mustache attached. In his hands was a three-inch-thick coral-pink binder full of papers.

He looked like he was completely off his rocker; no wonder Veronica was ready to give him the boot.

"You can close the door, Veronica," Kelly said.

Veronica gave her a look as though to say, *are you sure?*

Kelly nodded.

"I'm at my desk if you need me." Veronica shot Harry a distrustful glance as she pulled the door closed.

Once it clicked shut, Kelly came around the desk. "Mr. Townsend, I presume."

Hank smiled behind the disguise. "What gave it away?"

"That you're my ten a.m. appointment." She shot him a wink. "Otherwise, I would never have recognized you."

"Well, aren't you a saucy one."

Man, he had a great voice. Although in most of his movies, he sported an American accent, Kelly thought that they should utilize his real one. It was freaking hot.

"I am. Would you like to remove your hat and nose, so we can get started?"

Hank set the coral binder on her desk before he pulled the straw hat and glasses off. He dropped both items next to the chair opposite her, and getting her first in-person look at him was awe-inspiring. With bushy dark eyebrows, a full head of thick, black hair with just the hint of red, and stormy gray eyes, he was smoking. In a craggy, manly sort of way. Like he should be wearing a kilt and riding across the moors stealing lasses from their betrotheds.

Realizing she was being entirely inappropriate about a potential client, she held her hand out. "Kelly Barrow."

He gripped her hand in a firm pump. "Nice to meet you. Call me Hank."

"I will. You, of course, can call me Kelly." She went around to the back of the desk and flipped her planner open to take notes. "Now, I understand that you're paying for your younger sister's wedding?"

Hank took a seat in the empty chair across from her. "Yes, that's right. I want Julia to have the best and according to several friends of mine, that's you."

Kelly wanted to preen, but refrained. She'd built her business and reputation of being discreet while creating beautiful weddings for celebrities. There had been a few hiccups over the years, but overall, Something Borrowed Wedding Solutions's reputation was unblemished. Professional bridesmaids for the woman who needs an extra body, or someone to handle all the details her flaky cousin or workaholic best friend couldn't.

"That is lovely to hear. Is Julia in town with you?"

Hank picked up the binder and waved it at her. "No, but she gave me a list of demands…I mean, plans. Actually, it's more like a manual. Julia has rather simple tastes in decor."

His fond grin told her he was teasing, but she figured there was probably some truth in his words. Most siblings she knew had a love/annoyance relationship with each other.

"Julia's a model, right?" Kelly said.

"The new face of Ralph Lauren. She's on a photoshoot overseas now and I had some time between filming, so I figured I'd fly up here and get the ball rolling." He set the binder on the edge of her desk and sat back in the chair, his lips kicking up at the corners. "Besides, I'll admit, I was curious about you."

Kelly was sure she was blushing. "What about me?"

"What you were like in person. If you were really as charming as you seemed over the phone."

"And what have you decided?"

His stormy gray eyes were breathtaking. "I'd say more so, now that I've seen the entire package."

Kelly cleared her throat. "Are you flirting with me?"

Hank's deep chuckle was a toe-curler to be sure. "Normally women don't have to ask, but yes, I am."

Kelly reached out to grab the binder, avoiding his gaze as she set it next to her planner. "Well, then I suppose I should tell you the number-one rule here is to never date clients or their friends and family."

"Damn." Her gaze met his, surprised by his disappointed frown. "That puts a damper in my plans to take you to dinner. Perhaps we could call it a business meeting?"

Talk about charming, the man had an arsenal of the stuff. It was very hard not to laugh. "Considering I know where your head is, no I don't believe we could."

Hank stood up, leaning over the desk with what could only be described as a seductive look on his face. "I suppose I will just have to change your mind."

Kelly's heart pounded. It had been so long since someone had flirted with her. She'd been hit on and catcalled over the years, but an honest-to-God flirt fest?

Man, it felt good.

"You can try, but it's never going to happen."

"What's never going to happen?" Chris asked.

Kelly jumped to her feet and looked around Hank's shoulder. Chris stood in the doorway with a stack of papers in his hands, his hair perfectly in place and his suit pressed. The navy blazer drew attention to the swimmer's shoulders and deep V into his waist, indicating he had his suits tailor-made for his lean muscles. He worked the style so well, he should be modeling suits for Hugo Boss. He looked *that* good.

*Where the heck did that thought come from?* Kelly had always been aware that Chris was attractive, and as his normal attire consisted of formal suits and ties, it should be old hat seeing him like that.

It was probably just the high of Hank's interest that made Kelly aware of every man around. That was logical.

"Chris. I didn't hear you knock."

He cocked his head, watching her as though she'd lost her mind. "That's because I didn't. I brought the contracts for the new clients you had coming today. Since I was supposed to be here for this meeting, I figured it was okay to come on in. Sorry I was late, by the way."

God, had she sounded testy with him? By the confused look on his face she was guessing she had been. Usually, Chris dropped the contracts off and left, but since he was such a big fan of Hank's, she had agreed to let him come in and meet him.

"Yes, of course, I'm sorry. Mr. Townsend just wanted to maintain his privacy, so I had Veronica close the door behind her. Hank Townsend, this is Christian Ryan, the company attorney. Chris already knows you, since he's a big fan of your movies."

Chris held his hand out to Hank. "Mr. Townsend, a pleasure. I apologize for being late."

Hank released Chris's hand and beamed. "Thanks, man. And you haven't missed much, except me trying to convince Kelly to go to dinner with me."

Kelly watched Chris's eyes widen. "I see." Chris glanced her way, clearly asking her silently if she needed to be rescued.

She was a big girl, though and could handle a ladies' man like Hank Townsend. "I was just explaining to Hank that fraternizing is frowned upon at Something Borrowed."

Did Chris appear relieved? His shoulders sagged a little and the tense, awkward look from moments ago had disappeared.

"And Kelly is a stickler for the rules." Chris came forward, maneuvering around Hank, and set the thick stack of papers on her desk. "Here are the contracts I was dropping by, as I mentioned."

She must have imagined the emotion from him, because he acted completely chill now.

"Great. Thanks, Chris."

He hesitated, and Kelly waited for him to say something else.

"Was there more?" she asked.

"No, of course not." He took a few steps toward the door and turned, as though he'd remembered something. "Actually, I was just going to see if you were free for lunch?"

Kelly turned the page of her planner to her calendar and clicked her tongue. "I'm not. I can do tomorrow, though."

"Sure, that sounds great." Chris nodded at Hank, his hand on the doorknob. "Nice meeting you, Hank. You're in good hands."

Kelly noticed Hank wink at Chris before he said, "I'm pretty sure you're right."

Chris's smile seemed strained as he left and closed the door behind him. Kelly stared at the dark wood for a moment, wondering at Chris's air of irritation. She'd expected him to fawn all over Hank, but he'd appeared annoyed at the attention the actor had directed at her.

*He was probably just looking out for me. Afraid I'd get hurt.*

"So, you said no to dinner...but what about lunch?" Hank asked.

Kelly's attention centered back on Hank, and away from worrying about what her friend was thinking. "I just told Chris I was busy."

"Yeah, you told Chris, not me."

Kelly laughed as she sat back down again. "You're tenacious."

Hank arched a brow at her, his lips turned up in a wicked grin. "That's not a no."

*Oh yeah, I could get used to the attentions of this man.*

# Chapter 4

Chris threw all his weight behind the punch, knocking his bag back a good foot. He'd converted one of the three bedrooms in his house into a gym, equipped with a folding treadmill, weights, and a punching bag anchored from the ceiling. It was his sanctuary from the stress that could come with handling other people's affairs.

His muscles screamed in protest as he used a combination of jabs, dancing on the balls of his feet across the wood floor. Sweat rolled down his shoulders and back, his hair soaked against his forehead as he brought up his knee, watching his actions in the wall mirror he'd installed. He let out several loud grunts as he jammed his knee into the leather, holding it still as he pummeled it.

He'd left his office and driven straight home, antsy as hell and needing a good workout. He had no idea what had triggered the overwhelming urge to vent a little violence on his unsuspecting punching bag, but it felt good to let it out.

The blast of Panic! at the Disco flooded his ears through the bud speakers and he took a break to grab some water. The song was one of Kelly's favorites. Anytime it came on, she would scream the words at the top of her lungs.

As the cold water from his bottle traveled down his throat, he remembered the husky giggle he'd heard through the door of Kelly's office today as he'd left. It had struck him, especially since Kelly wasn't really a giggler. He couldn't remember the last time she'd laughed like that.

It hadn't taken him long to notice when Hank had flirted with Kelly, she'd blushed a rosy hue. It was the same color that appeared whenever a sex scene on a movie or TV show they were watching got steamy. Her hazel eyes had sparkled and although she'd looked at Chris when she'd spoken to him, her gaze flicked back to Hank.

She liked the guy, despite her protests about not dating clients. Chris could understand; most women would turn their heads at a famous actor asking them out, especially a handsome one.

But it had still thrown him that Kelly was susceptible to Hank's charms.

Chris poured some water over his already soaked head, a shock of cold causing a shiver when it touched his skin. The water hit the floor with a splat and he pulled a towel from the rack he kept on the far wall. He dropped it on the floor and mopped up the liquid with his foot, still brooding about the events in Kelly's office.

Once it was cleaned up, all the energy drained out of him. He needed to go shower and start some dinner.

It was his birthday, after all.

He was a little surprised that Kelly hadn't said anything. She never forgot his birthday, even when he wished she would. At least he wouldn't be put through any crazy party antics this year. The clown party for his thirtieth two years ago had almost given him a heart attack. Kelly had laughed uproariously at the terrified expression on his face every time one of the painted entertainers she'd hired approached him. It was pure wickedness on her part to tease him that way, but he'd gotten his revenge with the haunted house party he'd thrown a few months later. Half the guests had dressed up like zombies and Kelly had hardly left his side.

He loathed clowns and zombies freaked her out. What a pair they made.

Chris's phone beeped through the music and he pulled it out of his armband. Unlocking the screen, he saw it was a text message from Kelly.

*I don't wanna cook. Meet me at Shotguns?*

Shotgun Weddings Bar and Grill served the best burgers in Nor Cal, better than whatever crap he probably had in his fridge.

*Hell yeah.*

*Sweet. See you in a few. You're buying.*

*You asked me out.*

*Don't be a cheap ass. I'll get dessert.*

Chris laughed.

*Deal.*

He left his spare room, taking the wraps off his hands as he walked down the hallway. His knuckles ached already, telling him he'd overdone it tonight, but he still felt better than he had an hour and a half ago.

He reached his bedroom, where he kicked off his shoes and stripped out of his clothes. Chris was a neat guy who didn't like things out of place. Instead of leaving his laundry on the floor, he picked up the bundle up and tossed it into the wicker basket next to his shiny cherry wood dresser. Chris left the hand wraps on top of the dresser. He'd put those away later, since he wasn't likely to trip over them in the dark.

He walked past the king size bed with its gray comforter. The head and foot board perfectly matched his dresser and nightstands. On top of each were matching lamps with gray bases and eggshell shades. The right nightstand held his alarm clock and a picture of his parents on their wedding day. On the left was a photo of Kelly and him at one of the first weddings she organized.

Next to it was another frame of silver, with Ray in his dress blues and Chris with his arm around his friend's shoulders. They'd been celebrating Ray's boot camp graduation and it was no surprise that Kelly had been the one to take that picture of them.

The slight twinge in his chest hurt, mostly because it reminded him that he wasn't over losing his friend. Ray had been the brother he'd always wanted, a confidant that had his back and called him on his bullshit. As much as he tried to get out there with his other lawyer friends or guys he'd kept up with from college, they couldn't replace Ray.

Chris pulled the buds from his ears, determined not to settle into a downer mood on his birthday. When he set his phone on the counter in the connected bathroom and pulled the headphones from the jack, Green Day blared through the room. He'd bought the three-bedroom, two-bathroom house in Somerset as a foreclosure and had been slowly updating it himself. He'd started in the master bath and bedroom because he knew he'd be spending the most time in there and he loved the way his shower had turned out. It was tall and wide, big enough for four people with dual shower heads and dark gray tile. The toilet had a separate door, and the second sink on the double vanity sparkled compared to the one he used every morning. Cass hadn't spent the night much and when she did, she'd always used his side.

He turned the nozzle in the shower for the hot water, adjusting the cold slightly so he didn't peel his skin off. Finally, he stepped into the waterfall, sighing loudly as the tepid spray rained down on his body. He was too hot for his normal scalding shower, but the steady, massaging stream was still amazing.

The music on his phone paused and he heard the text notification. A sense of urgency shot through him, and he hoped Kelly hadn't changed her mind about going out for food. He finished scrubbing the sweat from his body and hair with body wash and shampoo. Once the soap was gone, he stepped out onto the black bath mat and grabbed his towel on the wall. Wrapping his towel around his waist, he went to the counter and unlocked the screen on his phone with his trigger finger.

*By the way. Happy Birthday, SBF.*

Attached was a picture of a clown holding a birthday cake, a wicked grin on its painted face. He grimaced.

*You're evil.*

*I love you.*

*I know.*

Chris shook his head with a grin and ran his hand over the steam-covered mirror. He went ahead and left the golden five o'clock shadow that had formed on his cheeks and chin. Kelly wouldn't care if he shaved or not.

He finished getting ready and left the house to climb into his slate gray Toyota Tundra. He blasted the radio as he pulled out onto the dirt road that would take him to highway 16. Pine trees lined the two-lane road, and in the distance, he could see the hills beyond growing taller. When he hit the three-way stop, he waved a red sports car on his right through before gunning the engine.

It took him about ten minutes to get to Shotguns, as it was on the other side of Sweetheart. All the businesses sported clever, wedding-themed names, like Bow Ties Italian Restaurant. It was what the small foothill town was known for. A private place that catered to celebrity weddings. It was where most of the revenue came from that kept the businesses booming. A picturesque oasis; a country setting with California sensibilities.

Chris pulled into Shotgun's lot and parked next to Kelly's truck, a sneaking suspicion crossed his mind. The parking lot was packed except for one spot right up front. Kelly forgetting his birthday?

He was an idiot.

He climbed out of the truck and walked up the steps to the dark wood building. The bouncer, Phil, grinned at him with his hand on the doorknob. The dark haired, six-foot-four body builder towered over him like Shrek, but with a better attitude.

"Any chance there isn't a surprise party waiting for me in there, Phil?"

"Sorry, pal, Kelly told me I'm sworn to secrecy."

Chris rolled his eyes. "Let's get this over with, then."

Phil opened the door and Chris walked into the bar, which was pitch black and eerily quiet.

The lights came on with an explosion of "surprise" and Chris's heart nearly propelled from his chest. Even though he had been waiting for it, he hadn't been fully prepared.

The ceiling of the bar had been run with streamers in primary colors, with white twinkling lights threaded throughout. On the bar sat brightly wrapped boxes and bags, a dozen of them at least. The circular tables that usually lined the edge of the dance floor were covered in blue table cloths and the centerpieces were Photoshopped pictures of Chris riding a unicorn.

Half the town of Sweetheart was there, smiling and cheering. At the front of the crowd of friends was Kelly, clad in blue jeans and a black sleeveless blouse. Her dark hair was swept up on top of her head and her wide, excited smile was too infectious not to return. She came over to him and gave him a big hug, wrapping her arms around his waist.

"Did I get you?"

Chris chuckled good-naturedly. "You got me until I pulled into the parking lot. Although, it was considerate to leave me a spot right up front for my birthday present, it was also highly suspicious."

"You're welcome. I figured I hadn't done a surprise party yet…had to do something cool for your big three two."

"Thirty-two is not a special birthday."

She gave him a tight squeeze. "Every Chris birthday is special."

Despite the cheesiness of the statement, it still warmed him to his core. Besides his parents, Kelly was the only family he had.

"Just as long as a clown never jumps out of my cake," he said.

"Oh, shoot, I meant to cancel that."

Chris growled and picked her up off her feet. "The unicorn-riding pictures were a nice touch. I appreciate the fact that I wasn't shirtless."

"If I hadn't invited your parents, that might have been the case."

Chris searched the crowd and found his parents at the edge closest to the bar. His mom was already halfway through a glass of white wine by the looks of it, while his dad held a glass of dark liquid in his hand.

"I'll run over and say hi."

Kelly untangled her arms from around him. "I'll go tell the kitchen we are ready to bring the food out."

"What are we having?"

"Bacon and avocado sliders, garlic fries, coleslaw, and fruit salad."

Chris nodded, his mouth watering eagerly. Shotguns sliders were like potato chips; you couldn't eat just one and although the garlic fries made your breath stink to high heaven, they were delicious.

He headed over to his parents, kissing his mom on the cheek first.

"Hey, guys. Thanks for coming."

"Of course. It's not every day my baby turns thirty-two." His mother sniffled and she pretended to dab at her blue eyes.

Chris snorted. "I'm hardly a baby."

"You know what they say. You'll always be *my* baby."

Chris's cheeks burned. As much as he loved his mother, having only one child had made him the center of her undivided attention. As a kid, it had been wonderful. As an adult, it was almost a curse.

"You two look great," Chris said, changing the subject. "Retirement obviously agrees with you."

It was true. Both of his parents were tan, and his mother's usual dark blond hair had been bleached by the sun. His mother was a retired teacher's aide and his father had managed the local Wells Fargo Bank until just a few months before. He'd thought that his dad would have gone nuts by now, but he smiled warmly, the lines by his green eyes crinkling.

His dad raised his glass to him. "Your mother has me doing yard work every day. Took me to Home Depot yesterday and cleaned out the garden center. I don't think there was a flower left in the whole place."

His mother scowled at him. "You are so full of dung noodle. I bought a couple flats for the flower beds under the windows. Hardly a dent in their inventory."

Chris smirked as his dad ran a hand over his sandy hair, which was a bit grayer since their last family dinner two weeks ago. "It was more than a few flats, dear. My wallet cried the whole way home."

"Oh, you." She tossed her head, but her blond bob had so much product it hardly moved. His mother ignored his dad and focused on him instead. "We were so glad that Kelly invited us. You know, I always thought she was a nice girl and would make *someone* very happy."

The pointed compliment was not lost on Chris, but he was not going to argue with his mother in the middle of Shotguns with half the town listening in. It wasn't as though he hadn't told her countless times before that Kelly and him were just friends.

His father placed his hand on Chris's mom's back, and shook his head. "Leave them be. If they are meant to be, then it will happen without you meddling."

"I don't meddle."

His father shot him a grin of conspiracy. "Don't worry, we won't be staying long. Just going to fill our bellies and take off. You have fun."

As his father led his protesting mother away, he was suddenly lost in a crowd of well-wishers buying him drinks. Every once in a while, he'd catch a glimpse of Kelly in the crowd and by the fourth shot, he was pretty loopy.

That had to explain why his mother's words kept haunting him.

*She would make someone very happy.*

Correction. Someone other than him very happy.

Why was that thought so depressing?

# Chapter 5

Kelly came around the side of her car several hours later, wishing she'd remembered to leave the porchlight on. Her two-story Lindal home was dark and the cobblestone path to the steps was barely visible in the sliver of moonlight from above.

She held onto the car and gingerly made her way around to the passenger side. Kelly stared down at the ground, watching for movement. The last thing she wanted was to step on a snake by mistake. It didn't matter what kind of snake; she was terrified of them all.

She opened the door to a very inebriated Chris grinning at her in the dome light, his short hair in disarray and his blue eyes heavy lidded.

"Happy birthday to me!" he sang.

Kelly laughed as she reached in to help him out. She grunted under his weight as she pulled him unsteadily to his feet.

"I think this was the best party you've ever given me."

Kelly held onto his waist to keep him upright. "I'm pretty sure that's the bottle of Jose talking."

He threw an arm around her shoulders and gave her a squeeze.

"Nope, it was all you. I appreciate it." He gave her a smacking kiss on the cheek. "Wait? What about my presents?"

"We'll grab them tomorrow." She led him up the walkway to her porch, ready to abandon him if anything slithered across the ground.

"You could have taken me home. I'd have been fine."

"I'd rather keep an eye on you." She'd already made up the spare room for him, knowing how he liked to tie one on. It was kind of funny to see her so serious, proper best friend get shit faced once a year on his birthday. The rest of the time, he stuck to beer or a glass of wine.

"You are the best friend a guy could ask for."

"Now you're making me blush."

She turned the knob on the front door, stumbling a bit as she balanced him. She pushed it open a crack and used their bodies to increase the gap when the door caught on her rug.

*I really need to find a better place for that.*

Kelly flipped the switch by the door and her living room lit up. Her cat, Pepper, lifted his black-and-white head from his position on the back of the large couch and yawned. He stretched his paws across the colorful quilt she always kept there, giving her otherwise brown-and-white living room a pop of color. She liked her furniture simple, and neutral, but made up for the boring palette with bright blankets and colorful paintings on the walls. She wasn't much of an art connoisseur; she didn't know what made a painting good or bad, she just bought what she liked.

Pepper watched them pass with sleepy eyes, before rolling onto his back...

And right off the couch. He landed on the wood floor with a plop and an affronted meow, as though it was Kelly's fault he was such a dork.

"Hey, I could have told you there wasn't enough room for tummy rubs."

Pepper sneezed and trotted into the kitchen, probably to hover by his food bowl. Although she'd fed him before she left, he was never satisfied.

"It is weird to talk to animals."

Kelly laughed. "You only say that because you don't have one. Believe me, if you got a dog or cat, you'd be just as crazy as the rest of us."

"Yeah, maybe. Speaking of crazy, I never told you, but I had a hefty crush on you in eighth grade," Chris said, abruptly.

Kelly stumbled in astonishment, slamming Chris into the wall just outside the guestroom door. The pictures that decorated the wall shook under the force as Chris grunted.

"Ow, geez, don't kill me!" he said.

Kelly leaned against the wall and stared up at him, completely thrown. "What did you just say?"

Chris met her gaze with his bleary blue eyes. "I said, I had a crush on you too, but Ray called dibs. So, I let him have you."

She spluttered with indignation. "You *let* him have me? Like I'm a freaking ball you two found on the playground? Because if you had told me that you liked me, I might not have gone with Ray?"

His mouth flopped open and shut like a fish trying to get air, his brain obviously not working at full capacity. "No, I just meant…I just didn't want to fight my best friend over a girl. You know, bros before—"

Kelly poked him in the stomach. "If you finish that sentence, I will drop you right here and let you sleep on the hardwood floor."

"I'm only saying he told me about his crush first, so I was the good guy and kept my mouth shut."

Still irritated with him, Kelly scoffed. "You know, good guys finish last, right?"

"That seems to be the truth, at least for me. I keep getting dumped." His expression drooped like a hound dog denied a car ride. "Why do you think that is?"

Kelly honestly didn't have a good answer for him. Chris was sweet, funny, successful, and all in all a great catch, when he wasn't saying stupid drunk shit. She had no idea why women kept letting him get away.

"Maybe it's because you still say things like 'bros before hos.'"

"Technically, I only *started* to say it. You *actually* said it."

His sloppy grin hit her right in the stomach, melting her irritation and leaving her giddy.

*Giddy? Where the hell had that come from?*

"All right, I'm going to put you to bed before you *do* say something that pisses me off."

She helped him through the doorway of the guest room and onto the bed. The minute his butt hit the comforter, he flopped back on it, staring up at her pensively.

"Did you ever think about it?" he asked.

She paused in the process of bending over to untie his shoes. "About what?"

"About you and me? If you hadn't gone out with Ray?"

Kelly's cheeks warmed up, and she was thankful she hadn't turned on the light or her blush would have given her away. "When you were a skinny, towheaded kid? Nope, not once."

"Hey, I was a little awkward! I wasn't *that* bad though."

No, he hadn't been bad at all. And she'd never said anything out loud, but, when Chris had approached her, she'd thought *he* was going to ask her out.

And she'd been a little disappointed when he didn't.

Not that she hadn't loved Ray. She had with all her heart. But she'd been a thirteen-year-old girl noticing boys for the first time and Chris, well...

Chris had been really, *really* cute in a nerdy way.

Kelly slid up next to him on the bed and leaned over to kiss his forehead. "No, you weren't bad, but there's no use wondering about it, is there?"

"I guess not." Before she could go back to removing his shoes, he grabbed her hand. "Hey, Kel?"

"Yeah?"

"What about that time sophomore year?"

Kelly's heart skipped several beats. "What time?"

"That winter break when you and Ray broke up for a few weeks."

She knew exactly what time he was referring to, but was surprised he was bringing it up, considering he'd acted as though she'd imagined it all. "What about it?"

"I don't know," he mumbled. "I just wonder…"

"What?"

Deep, even breathing was her only answer. Frustration ripped through her and for some reason, she wanted to shake him awake and ask him what he was about to say.

Instead, she finished with his shoes and grabbed the folded quilt from the end of the bed, spreading it out over his passed-out form. She left him to get a bottle of water and two Advil from the kitchen. Considering how he'd downed those drinks tonight, he'd need both in the morning.

Kelly flipped the light switch as she passed through the doorway. As she headed to her stainless-steel fridge first for the water, her mind drifting back to that December.

Right before Christmas break, Ray had picked a fight with her about something stupid. She couldn't recall what it was now, but she did remember him saying they should take a break. He was going with his family to Tahoe for the holidays, and he suggested they reevaluate things when he got back.

She'd been devastated and called her best friend, Jackie, but she hadn't picked up. Then, she'd called Chris, bawling her eyes out. They had never really hung out without Ray, but he'd shown up a half an hour later with junk food and DVDs. At first, he'd just held her while she cried, but after an hour or so, he'd given her a little shake and said, *"Don't stress about it, Kel. Ray is going to realize he's a moron and come crawling back."*

*"What if he doesn't?"* she asked.

*"Like I said…moron."*

Kelly smiled as she set the water bottle down on the counter and opened the cabinet to the left of the sink. She'd been mopey the first few days after Ray had left, but Chris had come by every day to take her on some adventure. They'd gone to Apple Hill, a stretch of road filled with pumpkin patches, craft fairs, and fabulous fall and winter treats. Before calling it a day they'd bought a pie, which they devoured with a half-gallon of vanilla ice cream as soon as they got back to her house. They'd been so sick the next day, neither one of them had left the house, but they'd still talked on the phone, both bitching and moaning about how much they ate.

The next day, once they'd recovered from their over indulgence, they'd gone to check out Christmas lights in Orangevale. They'd sipped hot chocolate as they'd walked along the sidewalk with other pedestrians, taking in the intricate light displays. By the time Christmas had passed and Kelly was actually having fun. Chris has taken her sledding. Dancing. Although Ray hadn't called her once, Chris had done his best to keep her from thinking about it and she'd appreciated it.

Kelly found the Advil in her medicine basket and opened the bottle up. Once she'd dropped two pills into the palm of her hand, she put the basket back and picked up the water bottle. Chris had done nothing but try and make her feel better forever, so she didn't mind helping to prevent his massive, post-birthday hangover.

The thought of drinking too much took her back to Will Yates's New Year's Eve costume party. Kelly had stopped feeling so sad about Ray by that time and had gone to the trouble of finding a mermaid costume to wear. Chris had shown up as James Bond in a black tux. He'd agreed to drive, so she could drink, and once they'd arrived, she'd hit the sauce hard. Midnight rolled around, and there were only about ten people left at the party, including her and Chris. Will, and a couple of other guys had given her sloppy, New Year's Eve pecks, but Chris hadn't kissed anyone. In fact, when they'd gotten in the car that night, he'd seemed pissed at her.

"Are you mad at me?"

"No, why would I be?"

"I don't know but you keep giving me the stink eye."

He hadn't said anything else until he'd reached her house, where he'd slammed the car into park. She remembered jerking forward with a cry, and turning to give him a piece of her mind, but stopped when she'd seen the expression on his profile as he stared out the windshield. His jaw stiff and his eyebrows slashed down over his eyes. She'd never seen him look like that before.

"You're right. I'm mad."

"Well, duh."

He'd turned in the seat to face her and even with the headlights off, she could feel the intensity of his gaze.

"I'm mad because *I* wanted to kiss you tonight. Instead, I stood around watching you kiss everyone else *but* me."

Going back to that moment, she could still remember the flash of shock, followed quickly by excitement and confusion. A part of her was thrilled by Chris's admission and she leaned toward him, her eyes fluttering closed.

Then someone knocked on her window and she'd jumped a mile in the air, thinking it was her dad...

Only when she'd opened the door, and the dome light flashed on, it was Ray on the other side. He'd been bundled up in a jacket and beanie, holding a bouquet of bright Gerbera daisies, her favorite flower, in his left hand and that beautiful, lopsided grin she loved on his handsome face.

*"Hey, Kel."*

Sluggishly, she'd climbed out of the car to face him, leaving the door open behind her. *"What are you doing here? It's one in the morning."*

*"I know. We came home a day early, and I just couldn't wait to see you. To tell you what an idiot I was. I am really, really sorry. I know I hurt you, but the distance made me realize how much I love you, Kelly. How wrong I was to think there was anyone else out there for me but you. Please, forgive me?"*

She'd stared at him, the light from inside Chris's car glistening off his dark skin. His eyes sparkled in the dimness, and Kelly's stomach flopped over. This was Ray. They'd been together two and a half years. He was her friend and her first love.

Behind her, Chris cleared his throat and when she turned around, he was standing in the open driver's side door. Smiling as though moments ago he hadn't been admitting to wanting to kiss her.

*"Glad you're back, buddy. I'll talk to you later, Kel."*

Kelly hadn't had a chance to even say bye before he was back in the car. She'd closed his passenger door, completely thrown for a loop by the roller coaster of the night's events. As he'd pulled out of her drive and his taillights had disappeared, she kept replaying his words in her head, even as Ray pulled her in for a hug.

It had felt good to be held by him again, but a lot had happened, and she needed time to consider what *she* wanted. She'd taken the flowers from Ray and told him she needed a few days to think. That she'd see him at school. He'd been disappointed, but he'd had two weeks to realize that he wanted to be with her. She was due some time.

After a weekend of stressing, she'd been at Chris's locker on Monday, waiting impatiently. Just before the bell rang he'd come up, and although she could have sworn something foreign flashed across his face, it was replaced to swiftly by his usual gamin grin for her to be sure. *"Hey, Kel."*

*"Hey."* She'd shifted from foot to foot in front of the blue aisle of lockers, drumming up the courage to be straight with him. *"Did you mean what you said to me on Saturday?"*

*"What?"*

*"About...about wanting to kiss me?"*

He'd opened his locker, blocking his face with the door. *"Honestly, Kel, we had been spending a lot of time together and I think I just...got caught up in the moment. Ray loves you and you love him. You two belong together."*

Was that relief or disappointment flipping her stomach over? Sixteen years later, she still couldn't say for sure. *"You didn't mean it, then?"*

He'd closed his locker, and looked her right in the eye. *"No, I didn't mean it."*

She'd turned and walked away, feeling like an idiot for obsessing about it all weekend. She'd gotten back together with Ray, and things had gone back to the way they'd always been.

Now, she stared down at Chris's sleeping form and wondered why in the heck he'd brought that up tonight? What had made him even think of it?

She set the pills and water down on the end table, and left the room, so many questions left unanswered.

*Maybe it's better that way. In the morning, I'll pretend he never asked, unless he brings it up. And even then, what's the point in wondering what might have been? Things are great now.*

No sense in spoiling a good thing.

# Chapter 6

Kelly woke up Sunday morning with a nasty, cottonmouth sensation and an ice pick headache stabbing sharply along the right side of her skull. God, it was as though she had the hangover, and she hadn't had a thing to drink.

She climbed out of her bed gradually, rubbing her stinging eyes as she stood with a wince. She'd tossed and turned most of the night, thinking about Chris and what the heck he'd meant about *if she ever wondered.* Wondered what? What would have happened if Ray hadn't been waiting for her? If she had wanted to kiss Chris too?

Ugh, her head hurt.

She used the bathroom and splashed her face with warm water. After she brushed her teeth and slipped a warm, comfy sweater over her short-sleeved pajama top, she padded barefoot down the stairs. The smell of bacon drifted from the kitchen, and she could hear Chris humming to himself as things sizzled.

How could he be so cheerful after how much he'd had to drink?

She stopped in the entryway and watched him flip a pancake over with a spatula. Wearing his jeans and T-shirt from last night, he looked rumpled and delicious.

*Delicious? Where in the world had that come from?*

Okay, she could admit that Chris was beautiful. He had broad shoulders and muscular arms that weren't overdone. His jeans hung low on his hips and she knew that his legs were sculpted and strong.

This was not something new. She'd always been aware that Chris was good-looking, but for some reason, she'd never really stopped to appreciate it. He was just...*Chris*. Not a slab of man meat to be ogled and drooled over, like Chris Evans.

He spun around, using the spatula as a microphone as he belted out the words to a Three Doors Down song, only to choke in mid lyric when he saw her.

"Hey, you're up!"

"You're perceptive," she said, dryly. "And you're chipper. Got any coffee made?"

"Already on my second cup, which is why I am feeling good." He came close and kissed the side of her head with a loud smack. "Plus, my amazing best friend left me medicine and water to cure my hangover."

"You must have a gut made of steel. I'd be puking until noon if I imbibed as much as you did."

"You're also smaller than me."

"I guess." She pulled away from him to grab a mug from the cupboard, silently cursing the unfairness.

Pepper sat off to the side, watching the stove as though he was waiting for Chris to drop something tasty for him. His black tail, tipped with white, swished across the off-white tile floor. His golden eyes didn't even flick her way when she said good morning.

"Have you been feeding him again?" Kelly asked, coming up alongside Chris.

"Not today."

Kelly presented him with her fiercest scowl. "You're contributing to the begging of a feline. This is a punishable offense."

Chris glanced over his shoulder at Pepper. "Sorry, tubs, but your mommy is being a tyrant."

Pepper's attention diverted to her, as if he understood that she was the barrier between him and delicious, fatty meat.

"Don't give me that look, it's for your own good."

The tuxedo cat simply sniffed at her and left the room, his tail swishing regally in the air.

"Nice, now he's mad at me."

Chris laughed. "It's a cat. He doesn't actually understand the words coming out of my mouth."

"Oh, he knows that I'm the reason he was denied table scraps and he'll be seeking revenge. Just watch, I'm going to find a massive hairball on my bed later."

Chris's golden skin turned green. "Woman, I am cooking! You're going to make me lose my appetite."

"You? Not possible." She noticed his hair was wet and breathed in. There was a clean scent of soap beneath the bacon. "Did you shower?"

"Yeah, why? I smelled rancid." He seemed defensive as he turned her way. "It's not like I used your thirty-dollar girly soap. I always keep stuff here for when I crash."

Kelly wasn't staring at him because she was worried he'd used her stuff. The image of naked, soapy Chris under a spray of hot water had popped unbidden into her head, rendering her momentarily speechless.

She shivered, trying to collect herself.

"I know. I just thought you might be worn out today and be grumpy."

"Actually, not at all. I'm pumped. And I can't wait to play with the new iPad my wonderful, generous best friend gave me."

"You're very welcome."

Kelly poured some black coffee into her cup and realized her hand was shaking. She tried to tell herself it was the lack of sleep affecting her motor skills and not the flashing image of her best friend naked in the shower that had rocked her nerves, but then she'd be a liar. Could her hormones be in overdrive due to the sexual starvation she'd been in for almost eleven years? Did her body just wake up like, *"Hello, all males in the vicinity, I am ready for mating!"*

She giggled out loud.

"What are you laughing about?" he asked.

"Nothing."

"Uh huh. I don't believe you."

She turned to face him, and found him watching her with an evil grin. She froze with her coffee cup halfway to her lips. "Don't."

"Don't what?" he said, innocently.

Kelly placed her mug out of the way. "Whatever you are thinking about doing to get me to talk, do not do it."

Chris put the pancake he'd been flipping on top of a large stack and set the spatula down. "See, but now you're challenging my manhood and I *have* to do it."

Chris held his arms out, the flour-covered tips wiggling at her, and he contorted his face into a slack-jawed, zombie impersonation.

"No! I hate that, and you know it," she squealed.

"Gah grr argh." He started lumbering towards her, making horrific sounds that would have won him a role on *The Walking Dead.*

And even though she knew it was a game, she ran. Did she love zombie movies? Yes. Did they scare the pants off her? Definitely. She didn't even like seeing people dressed as zombies on Halloween; she was too afraid any minute they would form a group and start chasing her.

Behind her, Chris closed the distance and wrapped his arms around her from behind. She shrieked as he buried his face in her neck and pretended he was eating her.

"Stop! Stop! I wasn't laughing at you, I swear."

Her scream was tinged with laughter, until Chris stopped growling against the side of her throat. Had his teeth just scraped gently below her ear?

Then, she was very much aware of his warm breath on her skin. The hard bands of his arms around her. The press of his chest and...

Oh, shit, Chris was turned on. The proof was pressing into her butt.

But it was her reaction to his arousal that was really a punch in the gut. She had this crazy urge to wiggle her ass, and tilt her head, giving him better access to kiss his way up the side of her neck. Maybe reach back to cradle his head as she turned her lips to his.

Chris pulled away from her, ending the fantasy and bringing her back to stone-cold reality. A reality where she had just imagined making out with Chris.

Something. Was. Very. Wrong. With. Her.

She cleared her throat, and turned to face him. Not meeting his gaze, she murmured, "I guess I'll head up and take a shower."

A few beats went by before he responded. "All right. I'll probably be gone when you get out. Got a lot of stuff to do today."

Why was this so awkward?

"Then I guess we'll talk later."

"Yeah. Enjoy your shower."

Kelly's gaze snapped up at the husky tone in his voice, but he'd already turned his back on her. He disappeared into the kitchen without a backward glance.

Kelly climbed the stairs, confusion bubbling in her stomach. Once she reached her bedroom, she shut the door and leaned back against it with a deep, shuddering breath.

She needed to start dating. If she didn't start getting some on a regular basis, she might do something stupid.

Like ruin an eighteen-year-long friendship.

# Chapter 7

"Kelly! You're not listening!"

Kelly jumped in her seat as her assistant, Veronica Torres, very nearly yelled at her.

"Sorry, what?"

"What is going on with you? You have been a space cadet for days!"

It was true, Kelly had been experiencing a rough time concentrating this week. There was just so much on her mind, both professionally and personally.

First, there was the Townsend wedding. She'd been going through everything for Hank's sister before their meeting on Friday, but the binder was massive. And although it helped that Julia was specific, her ideas were time consuming. For a multi-millionaire model, she was obsessed with do-it-yourself decorations. Every other paper inside was a print out of some craft with the Pinterest logo on the top. With a guest list of over two hundred and fifty people, she was going to have to enlist enough manpower to get the little Mason jar favors done.

On top of that Chris was being unusually quiet. She'd texted him to ask if he was coming over tomorrow for their Wicked Wednesday movie night and he'd told her he was meeting his lawyer friends for drinks instead.

It wasn't that she begrudged him time out with his colleagues. It just wasn't like him. Chris had never missed a WWMN, except for that one time he'd gotten the stomach flu, and this week was the one he chose to blow off? After what had happened over the weekend?

She should be understanding. She had other friends too, and they did spend a lot of time together. But there was a dark, niggling thought in the back of her head. A foreboding sense that things were changing between them and she didn't like it.

And it had all started right after she'd told him she was giving dating a go.

"Kelly!" Veronica cried.

Kelly shook her head. She'd gone and done it again! Veronica could be sharp with other people, but she'd never been anything but respectful to Kelly. Which was how it should be considering Kelly was *her boss*.

"You're right, I drifted off. I guess Tuesday feels like Monday." Kelly quirked a brow. "Still, I suppose you have a good reason for yelling at the one who signs your paychecks?"

Veronica's tan cheeks reddened, but her back straightened. Her dark eyes flashed with what Kelly could only imagine was determination. "I have been with you for the last six months as your assistant. You moved Wendy to consultant after three months of being your assistant and I would just like to ask for my chance."

"You want to be a bridesmaid?" Kelly wasn't surprised. Veronica was ambitious and hardworking. Bridesmaids pulled in a lot more money than assistants. But Kelly wasn't sure Veronica had the temperament to handle emotional clients.

"Yes, so much."

Kelly sat forward and put her folded hands on top of her desk. "I'm not going to lie to you. The reason I haven't thrown you into the game is because you can sometimes be a little too honest."

"Oh, believe me. I know that tact isn't my strong suit, but I am creative and detail-oriented. You know this."

"I do. But a big part of the business is pacifying difficult clients."

"Come on, have you had any complaints that I am anything but professional?"

"Well, he didn't complain, but the way you handled Hank Townsend wasn't great."

"The guy showed up in a stupid mask. I knew who it was, but he acted as though just the sight of his face was going to make all women in the vicinity swoon. Please." Veronica laughed.

Kelly put her boss face on and levelled Veronica with a stare. "And if he had been easily offended, he would have taken his money elsewhere."

All the sass went out of Veronica's sails and her laughter rang a little bitter. "You're right. I'm sorry. Man, this is not how I wanted this conversation to go."

"Lucky for you, I'm all for giving second and third chances. What else do you bring to the table as a wedding consultant?"

Veronica's face lit up with hope. "I think quickly on my feet. I'll even bring a client on, as my test run."

"And who is that?"

"My cousin, Teresa Valdez."

Kelly's heart tangoed with excitement. "Teresa Valdez from *Mi Loca Familia*?"

Veronica smiled as though she knew Kelly was already hooked. "Yes."

Kelly sat back in her chair, steepling her fingers like a supervillain. Teresa Valdez had been a new face in Hollywood three years ago and had broken out with the lead in the hit telenovela show, winning several awards that first year, and raking them in ever since. She was very much in demand, getting roles in two blockbuster hits this year. The girl would be a feather in Something Borrowed's cap and Veronica knew it.

*Clever girl.*

"I didn't know she was getting married."

Veronica danced in her chair excitedly. "They wanted to wait until after the season finale. They're keeping it under wraps."

"Who is the groom?" Kelly asked.

"Alejandro Garcia."

Kelly burst out laughing. "The guy who plays her brother on the show?"

"Thus, the secrecy."

"Yeah, I imagine that the studio heads won't like it."

"Well, there's more. Teresa is about six weeks pregnant, and if my very traditional aunt and uncle find out, they are going to flip their lid."

Kelly lost her smile. "So…this is literally a shotgun wedding?"

"Pretty much, except Teresa is holding the shotgun instead of her parents." Veronica pulled something up on her phone and turned it to show Kelly. It was a Pinterest board filled with beautiful wedding pictures of cakes, dresses, and decorations. "They want to have a large, traditional wedding in a Catholic church…before she starts showing."

Kelly scrolled through the pins. The cakes were tiered with bright colored flowers cascading over the fondant. A bride and groom wrapped together in a rope. Beautiful dresses with lace and ruffles.

She handed Veronica back her phone. "So, what's your plan?"

Veronica's eyes widened. "You're going to let me?"

"I haven't said so yet, but I'm asking…with about six weeks to plan, what are your ideas for accomplishing the details? How big of a wedding are we talking? How many people?"

"About three hundred."

Kelly almost winced, but held her expression passive. "Bridesmaids?"

"Seven, including me."

Kelly hated rushed affairs, especially giant ones. Something always went wrong. Last summer it had been her top consultant, Marley, falling in love with the best man of a wedding she was working. The bride also turned out to be unstable, and the whole thing had been called off anyway. However, Kelly had learned to look at the situation more closely and not just the zeros on the checks.

At least letting Veronica take the lead on her cousin's wedding was a good jumping off point to how she'd be in the field. Kelly just needed to lay down the rules. "I'll agree to taking your cousin on, if you come to me with a detailed plan by the end of the week."

"Oh, my God, thank you—"

"I'm not finished," Kelly said firmly. The excitement in Veronica's eyes dimmed as she continued, "I do not care if you two are family, you will treat her as though she were a client you had never met before. That means with the utmost respect and patience."

Kelly could tell by the expression on Veronica's face she was holding her annoyance with Kelly in check, but that was good. It meant she was learning. "Of course."

"I would also like to meet her before I agree to take her on as a client."

"Deal." Veronica held her hand out to Kelly, who took it in a firm shake. "She's actually here."

Kelly arched one perfectly manicured brow at her. "Like, here in town or in the building?"

"She's sitting out at my desk. I knew you didn't have any meetings this morning, so I thought if this went well, we could squeeze her in."

Kelly had to hand it to her; she'd played her hand well. "You're diabolical, Ms. Torres. Show her in, please."

When Veronica jumped up, her floral skirt and loose black top seeming to spin with her as she practically floated for the door.

Kelly held up a halting hand. "And Veronica?" Her assistant froze with her hand on the knob. "You're going to need to put an ad out for a new assistant for me. If you're planning this wedding, you won't have time to handle my schedule too."

Veronica flashed her a dazzling smile over her shoulder. "I'll get right on that, boss."

As soon as she disappeared, Kelly checked her cell phone, but there were no messages from Chris. Only an emoji-filled text from Hank with a glass of wine, a smiley face, and hands clasped together.

> *Drinks tomorrow?*

Kelly pursed her lips.

> *You really don't know how to be professional, do you?*

> *I am an actor. I can be whatever you need me to be. Just say yes.*

Kelly's fingers flew over the screen.

> *Maybe.*

There was a knock on her open door and Kelly put her vibrating phone face down on her desk and stood. Teresa Valdez walked through her doorway in a blue dress, her dark hair curled and flowing down her shoulders. She was curvy and gorgeous with full, lush lips and luminous dark eyes.

She was going to be a beautiful bride.

"Ms. Valdez, won't you come in? We have so much to discuss."

"Thank you for seeing us."

Kelly saw the *us* standing in the hallway, dancing from foot to foot nervously. Alejandro Garcia was tall and muscular, the sleeves of his red polo stretched tight over his biceps. A day's worth of scruff covered his square jaw, and his dark eyes shifted above his hawk-like nose.

"It's my pleasure. Won't you both come in and have a seat." She stood up and took first Teresa's soft one and then Alejandro's callused palm. When they were seated across from her, she silently thought they looked perfect together.

"I understand that we are working in a time constraint for your wedding."

Teresa nodded. "About a month."

Kelly glanced between them in surprise. "I thought you were only six weeks."

"Yes, but the women in my family show early and it all pops out in the front. Even with an empire waist dress, it's going to be obvious to my *abuela*. She had eight children of her own, and always could tell when my mother and aunts were pregnant, even before they were showing. It was as though she could smell it on them."

Kelly bit the inside of her cheek to keep from laughing at the imagery of her grandmother sniffing women and announcing, *"Yes! You are pregnant!"*

"And you're fine with your cousin running point?"

"Of course. V and I grew up more like sisters. I trust her with my life."

"Excellent. I will help her out, if that's all right with you. It's a big job and since it is a rush…"

"We understand and are willing to pay whatever you want to be discreet."

"Of course." Kelly pulled out her pink planner and flipped several pages in until she found a blank cluster. She made a to do list, numbering the items as they came to her. "Do you think you could have your invitation style chosen by this afternoon?"

"Absolutely. Veronica has all of my preferences."

"Good. If you send me a guest list complete with addresses by Friday, we can get the invitations out Monday." Kelly would have to call in a whole lot of favors, but she was the best. To be on top, you had to be willing to go above and beyond.

Teresa clapped her hands. "Fantastic. Thank you."

"You are most welcome. I'll talk to my attorney and have him draw up the contract. Where are you staying?"

"The Love Shack Hotel." Alejandro spoke for the first time, a wry smile on his face.

"Excellent. You two go rest and Something Borrowed will handle everything."

As the two left her office, Kelly spun around in her chair, her phone in her hand. A new text message from Hank waited for her, but still nothing from Chris. Stabbing at the letters on the phone, she tapped out a message for him.

*Can we talk?* She added a prayer emoji and a crying face emoji, and hit send.

With a sigh, she laid her phone face down on her lap. She couldn't force Chris to talk to her, but it made no sense for him to ignore her. They were still friends.

At least, she hoped so.

# Chapter 8

On Wednesday, Chris was ready to pick Mr. Kenneth Bruch up by the back of his expensive suit and toss him out on his rear. As the owner of Bruch Grocery, he was ruthless and sharp. As much as he respected the wily old man's head for business, his social skills left something to be desired.

Especially when it came to women.

"As your attorney, I would strongly recommend that you apologize to Ms. Langley and we settle out of court."

"I didn't do anything but speak the truth."

Chris calmly sang "Every Rose Has Its Thorn" to himself as a calming mechanism, holding onto his patience by a hair. "No. What you did was tell a nursing mother that if she wanted to"—Chris picked up the official court documents and read them verbatim—"*milk her udders like a dairy cow, she could do so on her own time.*"

"That woman chose to have a child and come back to work six weeks later. She was in the break room every hour with that machine hooked up to her…" Mr. Bruch held his wrinkly, liver-spotted hands in front of his chest. "You get my meaning. She'd be in there for twenty minutes every hour. It wasn't fair to the rest of the employees or me, for her to be sitting around on company time."

Chris didn't try to reason with the man's common decency or sense. Instead, he set the papers down and leveled the old man with a hard stare. "Ms. Langley has multiple witnesses, employees at your store, who are willing to testify on her behalf that she clocked out for the ten extra minutes she took on top of her ten-minute break, so she did not waste company time. They also maintain that she pumped every two hours, not every hour as you claim. And, there are several sworn statements that you sexually harassed and bullied Ms. Langley in front of other employees and customers."

Chris stood up, getting into his speech. "Now, if you don't settle and decide to take this to court, you will be going up against a nursing mother trying to do best by her child. You will be the big, bad corporate giant who bullies and harasses women. This is not the kind of image your company needs now. So, as your lawyer, I would suggest that you apologize to her, offer a generous pension package, and I will draw up the non-disclosure agreement for her to sign. Or you can take your chances and have your company's name splashed through the news." Chris sat on the edge of the desk, leaning over Mr. Bruch. "How sure are you that if this complaint goes public, other women won't come out of the shadows? You know what they say. If one person says it, then it's just a rumor. Two and it's gospel."

Mr. Bruch stood angrily, picking up his briefcase from the floor. "I thought I was paying you to be my lawyer and get me out of these things."

"You pay me to give you the best legal advice I'm able, and that is exactly what I am doing. If you do not value that advice, you can fire me and try your hand with someone else."

For a half a beat, Chris thought the old coot was going to go through with it. In the end, Mr. Bruch just mumbled, "Get an offer and agreement drawn up and I'll sign it."

Chris nodded as Mr. Bruch shuffled out the door. The minute Chris closed it behind the man, he let out a shaky groan.

For the most part, his client list consisted of kind, fair-minded businessmen and women.

And then there was Mr. Bruch, who made Ebenezer Scrooge look like Gandhi.

Chris went around his desk and picked up the phone, dialing out to the receptionist for Ryan and Parker Law Office. Although, at this point it was just Chris; Alan Parker was semi-retired and came back every two weeks to check up on things. Otherwise, he was down in Mexico at his beach house, soaking in the sun.

Maggie Crane picked up on the second ring. "Yes, Mr. Ryan?"

"Hey, Maggie. You can knock off for the day. I'll be heading out myself."

"Sounds good. Have a good night, sir."

Even though Maggie was only a few years younger than Chris, she still insisted on calling him sir. It made him feel old.

Chris packed up his papers and closed the office, pulling the shades and locking doors. It was a little after six and Chris was ready for drinks with a few of his lawyer friends. Although, he did feel guilty for bailing on

Kelly, he needed one night to not think about what had transpired between them over the weekend.

He walked through the door of Poor Red's Bar-B-Q in Diamond Springs seventeen minutes later, and saw several of his friends sitting in the back of the dark tavern. Rachel Quincy waved wildly at him, her face split into an excited grin. Trevor Grayson, Maria Hernandez, and Michael Vance turned in their seats and greeted him warmly as he sat down.

"Anyone else need a drink?" Chris asked.

"We started without you, buddy," Trevor said. He picked up the pitcher in the middle of the table and poured Chris a pint. He handed it to Chris and pushed his glasses up his slim nose. Trevor was two years older than Chris and weighed a buck fifty soaking wet.

"You had a bad day?" Rachel watched him with bright blue eyes. Her golden blond hair was twisted up in a firm bun, drawing attention to her delicate features. Chris wasn't oblivious to Rachel's interest; they had just never been available at the same time.

*Well, we are now. I should ask her out.*

"It was okay, just long. Lots of contracts to go over. And one pain in the ass client who can't seem to stay out of trouble."

Maria grimaced, her rather large nose wrinkling. Her curly dark hair was pulled back into a ponytail and she still wore her stiff, blue blazer. "Speaking of clients who can't stay out of trouble, at least you didn't have to stand there like an ass when your client doesn't show up for court."

"Ouch, that's rough." Michael was the oldest, in his mid-forties with salt-and-pepper hair and cool green eyes. He was also the quietest of their little group.

Michael and Maria were criminal defense lawyers, while Trevor practiced divorce and Rachel worked in child advocacy. Chris was the only one who specialized in business.

Trevor held up his beer, his Adam's apple bobbing in his skinny neck. "To our clients, who annoy us to no end, but without them, we'd be broke."

"Here, here," Michael said.

Chris took a healthy swallow of his beer and set the mug down on the table. Then the chatter kicked up. Maria asked Trevor about his girlfriend, who he'd been talking about proposing to since the week after he met her. They'd convinced him to give it six months at least, and the guy had listened. They were coming up on their one-year anniversary and Trevor was planning to pop the question right before.

Michael got up to refill their pitcher, leaving the chair next to Chris empty. He was about to pull his phone out of his pocket to check for messages, but Rachel took Michael's seat and gave Chris a dazzling smile.

"So, what's new?" she asked.

"Nothing." She leaned against the table and he couldn't help but notice the first several buttons were unbuttoned, showing off a generous hint of cleavage. "Got dumped last week."

Rachel's jaw fell open in obvious shock, a definite boost to his ego. "What? Why?"

Chris shrugged. "We just grew apart I guess."

"Well, it's her loss."

She patted his knee with a light caress. Her cherry red lips curved into a flirtatious smile. All the signals were there, and Chris knew that if he was going to ask her out, this was his in.

"Thanks, I appreciate that. Hey, Rachel, I've been thinking—"

His phone buzzed in his pocket, and he broke off.

"You were thinking what?" Rachel asked eagerly.

Chris pulled out his cell, giving her an apologetic smile. "Sorry, give me one sec. I just have to make sure it's not an emergency."

"No worries."

Chris did like the dimple in her left cheek and she was nice. He checked the screen and saw it was another text from Kelly.

*What in the hell is going on with you?!*

Chris winced. She'd even added an angry emoji and a middle finger emoji. Things were escalating and if he didn't want her showing up at his place to bawl him out, he needed to call her. He just wasn't sure what to say.

*Hey, Kel. Sorry for getting turned on and pushing my dick against your ass while we were wrestling. Wanna be friends still?*

Chris could chalk his reaction to Kelly up as a simple biological reaction. But that didn't explain wanting to kiss her neck. To cover her breast with his palm and knead her flesh. To slip his hand between her legs and play with her until she was limp and moaning.

His reaction and train of thoughts combined was what had him avoiding her like a giant sissy. Just like high school, when Ray had come back that winter break and he knew he'd lost his chance. He'd written it off as a symptom of spending too much time with Kelly and kept his distance, making sure never to be alone with her. It had helped, and things had eventually returned to normal.

Now, they were adults, although she'd probably tell him he wasn't acting like one.

His phone alerted him again that another message had come through.

*Stop being a child and answer me!!!*

"What's wrong?" Rachel asked.

Chris slipped his phone back into his pocket without replying to the texts. He'd call her when he got home. "It's just Kelly. She's mad at me because I skipped out on our weekly movie night."

"Kelly. Right, your lifelong best friend." She said it with a weird tone, as though that wasn't the real story.

He cocked his head. "Yeah, since we were thirteen. You've met her."

"I have. And I think it's nice that you two are so close. Most people assume that guys and girls can't be friends without some kind of emotional or physical complication, but not me."

Chris studied her expression, noticing that her voice had gone about an octave higher, something his clients did when they were lying about something.

"We definitely are *just* friends. Completely platonic."

*Shit. Did my voice just crack?*

"Mmmm...that's great." Rachel stood up. "I'm going to go use the restroom. Be right back."

She grabbed her purse from her original chair and headed for the dimly lit hallway, completely throwing him for a loop. One minute she was flirting with him and the next, she was running away.

Or she just really had to pee.

He turned to find Maria and Trevor watching him.

"What? Why are you two looking at me like that?"

"Nothing. Everything okay?" Trevor asked.

"I think so. We were just talking, and she suddenly had to go pee."

Trevor grinned at Maria slyly before addressing him once more. "Did you bring up Kelly?"

"Yeah, why?"

Trevor held out his hand to Maria. "Pay up."

"Shit." She laid a five-dollar bill in Trevor's hand.

Whatever they'd bet on clearly had something to do with him and Kelly, and irritation pricked across his skin like a thousand needles sliding in. "Somebody want to fill me in?"

Maria rolled her eyes. "We made a bet."

"Yeah, I got that. What about?"

They looked at each other again, as if silently rock-paper-scissoring who would break whatever news they had to him.

Maria apparently drew the short straw.

"Chris, Rachel has liked you forever," Maria said. "When I told her that Cassidy broke up with you, she was really excited."

She paused, and he held his hands up helplessly. "Okay, still not seeing the issue."

"It's Kelly," Trevor broke in.

His eyebrows fused together. "What about Kelly?"

"You are not that dense." When all he did was blink at Maria, she sighed heavily. "Or, maybe you are. Chris, come on. No woman wants to play second fiddle to another and with you, Kelly always comes first."

"What? That's ridiculous." *It was... right?*

Maria glanced over his shoulder. "Look, Rachel is coming back. Do not misunderstand me, I like Kelly. But if you ever want to have a functioning relationship with a woman other than her, you're going to need to take a step back from your BFF."

Chris wanted to say more, that they were wrong, but he didn't want it to be awkward for Rachel, so he snapped his mouth closed. He knew that women in his past had been jealous of Kelly, but was their friendship really scaring them off?

Rachel came back to the table, and sat back in Michael's chair. She looked around at them, as though sensing that some serious subjects were covered while she was absent. "What are you all talking about?"

Chris pushed his beer away, his mind racing. "I was just telling these guys that I need to get home. I'm wiped."

Disappointment flashed across her face. "Really? You just got here."

"I've got another half an hour drive and I don't want to get sleepy behind the wheel." He stood up just as Michael came back to the table and set another pitcher down.

"Hey, you're taking off?" Michael asked.

"Yeah, I'm going to call it a night." He pulled out a twenty and put it on the table. "Next round is on me."

Maria shot him a chiding look, as if to say, *why are you running away?* Trevor just tapped his fingers to his forehead in a salute.

"Bye, Chris," Rachel said, softly.

He patted her shoulder lightly. "See you, Rach."

The rest of his friends murmured their goodbyes and he took off. He headed for the door, his mind whirling as he thought back on all the relationships he'd been involved in since moving back to the area. Had he really put Kelly before all of them? Even if he had, she was his friend. Would things be different if she was a guy and had needed his help for something?

For him, not at all, but according to Maria, her presence in his life was scaring off potential girlfriends. All because of her gender.

He climbed into his car with a laugh.

*Screw that.* If he met the right girl, it wouldn't matter who his best friend was.

*Except if things were really platonic, then why did I nearly round third base wrestling with her the other day?*

It was the question that had been plaguing him for days. Sure, he'd gotten a boner before, but never like that. He'd almost slid his hands from around Kelly's waist and gripped her hips, pulling her body harder against him. Placed kisses along the soft skin of her throat and whispered dirty things in her ear. The whole fantasy had lasted only a moment, but it had lingered. He could still remember the sweet scent of her lotion; he knew it was lotion because Kelly didn't wear perfume. The hitch in her breath…

He'd pulled away, afraid she'd freak if she knew what he'd been thinking. He'd gotten the hell out of there and now, he had no idea how to pretend he hadn't thought about taking things to the next level with her.

Just like after that New Year's Eve party in high school.

He'd played it off like he hadn't meant what he'd said about kissing her, but he had. He'd wanted to kiss Kelly so bad it had hurt. He'd avoided her and Ray for weeks after, trying to push down the disappointment and frustration and eventually, it had worked and they'd gone back to being friends.

Now here he was, screwing everything up again.

Maybe taking a step back from Kelly was the best thing he could do right now. And in a week, he'd call Rachel and ask her on a date.

The drive back to Sweetheart was a two-lane curvy road, with tall pines on either side that would open briefly to grassy hills. The sun was still setting, and turned the sky the color of a ripe peach. He did love the area, and preferred the simple sounds of crickets and wildlife to the horn honking bustle of the city.

Chris turned down his driveway twenty-five minutes later, and tore down the gravel road. Once he parked inside his garage, he climbed out of his truck and went inside.

He passed through the small, simple kitchen and breakfast nook without bothering to flip on the light. Chris was pretty clean and organized, so he didn't worry about stepping on anything on the floor he might have forgotten about. The living room was barely a blip on his consciousness as he headed down the hallway to his bedroom.

Normally, he'd stay up and watch something on TV until he fell asleep, but he just wanted to go to bed. To clear his mind and not dwell on women or Kelly or why in the hell he was single.

Before he got ready for bed, he shot off a text to Kelly.

> *Hey, sorry, wasn't ignoring you. Just had a rough day. Not up for talking. Off to bed. Will text tomorrow. Night.*

Chris put his phone on vibrate and stripped down to nothing. He downed some ZZZQuil to aid the sleeping process. Then, he crawled under the covers and took a deep breath, trying not to think of anything heavy. His brain grew fuzzy and before long, he was drifting off to sleep.

Chris found himself in the middle of a crowded dance floor, surrounded by couples swaying to a slow country song. All of it was eerily familiar and he realized as he pushed through the wall of bodies that he was at his senior prom in the Sacramento Hilton Ballroom. Streamers, twinkling lights, and giant silver stars decorated the dark ceiling. It was supposed to create the illusion of a "Starry Night," which was the theme they'd voted on three months earlier.

He looked for his date, Zoe, but she was too busy making out with her ex-boyfriend in the corner.

Fan-freaking-tastic.

Even in his dreams, he still didn't get the girl.

Chris headed over to the separate room with linen-covered tables to sit. When he walked through the archway, he realized the room was now completely empty except for Ray. Even the cheesy love song had evaporated, leaving an almost chilly silence.

Ray sat facing him on the other side of a white table covered in half-eaten chicken and steak dinners and a beautiful flower centerpiece with silver stars poking up between the white roses. Ray looked just as he had that night. He'd had his mom braid his afro, creating clean even rows on his scalp. He was decked out in a white tux, his top hat sitting on the chair next to him. It was funny that before high school, Ray had been the shy one, and Chris the extrovert. Not anymore.

Ray nodded at him. "Hey, man, where's your date?"

Chris sat down next to the hat chair and sighed, forgetting for a minute this had all happened before. "Getting back together with her ex, apparently."

"That sucks. I'm sorry."

"It's okay. I knew that they had just broken up and I was an idiot to ask her." He looked around, noticing several men in the corner breathing fire. Another was doing back hand springs from table to table, drawing nearer and nearer.

Chris frowned when a couple of clowns raced by on mini bikes. "Where's Kelly? And I thought our theme was Starry Night? Why are those guys tossing torches at each other?"

Ray ignored his question about the performers and lifted a water glass in his hand. "Kelly is most likely at home. Probably sleeping."

Chris was surprised by how casual Ray was about it. "What? Kelly wouldn't ditch you."

Ray shook his head. "I ditched her, remember?"

Chris frowned. Ray had never deserted Kelly on a date. Besides his one crisis of adolescence their sophomore year, Ray had been the perfect boyfriend. At least, according to Kelly.

With a wry smile, Ray opened his white jacket and four red circles formed on the white dress shirt beneath. Blood ran down from the holes, turning his suit crimson.

"Are you up to speed now?" Ray asked.

Chris stared at him, horror flashing through his body as rationality broke through fantasy. "You're dead."

"That I am." Ray pulled his jacket closed, then brought the water glass he'd been holding to his lips. "But forget about my problems. Your love life sucks, right? How can I help fix it?"

Chris wasn't about to tell his dead best friend that all his relationships seemed to fail because of his friendship with Ray's former fiancée.

Or that he'd recently been fantasizing about her naked.

Ray set his glass down and waved his hand casually. "If you're worried I'm going to get mad about you using Kelly to chase girls off, don't be. If you two want to live in a lonely little bubble for the rest of your lives, more power to you. I just think you aren't being fair to each other."

"What do you mean?"

*Ray sat back in his chair, pushing the front legs off the ground. "I mean that neither one of you are moving on with your lives. You have your careers and each other, but where is the love? The happiness? What else do you have?"*

Ray's observations hit too close to the points Trevor and Maria had been trying to make.

"I had a girlfriend."

His friend scoffed. "Who dumped you. I knew that was going to happen, but not you. You actually thought she was going to share her dessert with you?" Ray laughed uproariously before ending his mirth with a sigh of, "Dumbass."

Chris's hackles rose in defense. "So, I missed the signs. It happens."

"Not if you're actually taking an interest in another person, but let's move on."

"No, wait, did you just call me selfish?" Chris asked.

"Oblivious, actually, but let's forget that for a moment. Anything else you want to share? Something that's got you down?"

He hesitated, but figured if Ray already knew that Chris was failing as a boyfriend, he probably had caught the rest of their little dramas.

"Kelly said she's going to start dating."

Ray nodded. "I know. I've been waiting for her to move on for years."

"Does it hurt?"

He seemed confused. "I don't really feel pain here. I mean, consciously, I know that means she's going to fall in love again, but all I feel is...content. What about you? You can't rely on Kelly to be your stand-in any longer."

"She's not my stand-in! We're just friends and sometimes, I prefer her company to anyone else's."

"You ever thought about the deeper reason why that is?"

A clown stood alongside them, blowing up long, sausage-style balloons and tying them together. Chris shrank away. If this was a dream that included clowns, he waited for it to turn into a nightmare. For the white-faced creature to attack him.

The high-pitched shriek of the latex rubbing against each other was like nails on a chalkboard. The clown handed Chris a colorful array in the shape of a heart and blew a kiss before skipping off.

Chris showed the heart to Ray, who held up his hands. "I don't know what the hell it means. We're in your brain, not mine. Now, how about you stop avoiding my question and give me a straight answer?"

"A deeper reason for why I prefer Kelly's company? Because I am comfortable with her?" Ray rolled his eyes and Chris stiffened. "Look,

*I've already decided to give Kelly some distance and I'm going to ask someone out. I've got it handled and you don't have to worry about us."*

Ray frowned. *"I'll always worry about you guys. You're my people. I just want you to know that I'm watching, and you need to figure out what you want before it's too late. Remember, tomorrow isn't promised."* Ray stood up with the lapels of his jacket clutched in his hands, showing off the bullet wounds as he spun around with flourish. *"I'm proof of that."*

Chris woke up with a start, staring up at his white ceiling as his chest heaved.

What in the hell was that? He'd had dreams of Ray before, but never like that. It was vivid and weird.

*Remember, tomorrow isn't promised.*

Chris covered his eyes with his arm, trying to calm his racing heart.

There was no way he was getting back to sleep now.

# Chapter 9

It was Friday night and Kelly sat next to Hank at the bar in Bow Ties Italian Restaurant. She'd suggested the dim, calm atmosphere rather than the bustle of Shotguns. The area had several booths lined up against the walls of the restaurant, with a few round tables in the middle. In another dining area closest to the kitchen, rectangle tables and booths filled the well-lit area designated for families. In the dark barroom, couples sat on the same side of the table, snuggled up and gazing at each other over wine and garlic bread.

Kelly had opted to sit at the bar because Hank was less likely to try to get cozy on the uncomfortable bar stools.

Another reason she'd chosen Bow Ties was because she was less likely to bump into Chris here, a plus since she was so agitated with him. The bar area was thinning out now that it was getting closer to nine o'clock, as people headed to more lively activities.

Kelly glanced at her phone again, but there was still no answer from Chris. Besides a few *"Sorry, just really busy"* texts, it had been radio silence. He always had his phone on him, so he had to be avoiding her. The bastard. She was going to kick his ass until he told her what the hell his problem was.

*Maybe he sensed my lustful thoughts and is scared I'll jump him.*

Which was ridiculous. She wouldn't jump Chris and ruin what they had. She had self-control. She was a freaking adult, unlike some people!

"Everything all right?" Hank asked.

Kelly set her phone on the bar face down and smiled, pushing away her turbulent thoughts.

"Yeah, just making sure there are no crises I'm missing."

Hank leaned an elbow on the counter, his gray eyes luminous in the low lights. "Ah, for a minute there, I thought you might be waiting for a rescue."

"Come again?" she asked.

He flashed a grin at her. Tonight, he was wearing a blue button-down and jeans, looking relaxed and stylish all at once. "You know. Women have their girlfriend call and say there's an emergency, so they can escape a horrible date."

Kelly picked up her glass of Merlot and took a sip. "I have no reason to do that."

"Because you're enjoying my company so much?"

"No, because this isn't a date," she countered.

Hank chuckled. "A few more nights out with me, and I'll change your mind."

"You're bordering on cocky, sir." Kelly crossed her legs as she sat on the barstool, noticing the way Hank's gaze drifted down to admire her limbs. She'd broken out her black dress with the loose skirt. She loved the way it swished around her legs when she walked, and the simple spaghetti straps showed off her neck and shoulders.

Not because she was trying to entice Hank. She just wanted to feel pretty. To enjoy the attentions of a handsome man.

There was nothing wrong with that.

Except her hand itched to check her phone again.

*I need to stop thinking about Chris. If he wants to be a dumbass over a little body malfunction, that's on him.*

"I prefer the term charming to cocky," Hank said,

Concentrating on the dimple in his cheek, she smirked. "I'm sure you do."

"I like that you're quick witted."

"As opposed to just laughing at everything you say?" she asked.

"Actually, yes. I don't get very many women who tell me no."

"Shocker."

"I didn't mean that I'm a man whore."

Kelly laughed. "This conversation is swiftly going south."

He took her hand in both of his, startling her as he met her gaze eagerly. "Then tell me more about you, Kelly."

His hands were warm and soft around hers, but besides feeling a little nervous, his touch didn't make her heart race. "Um, not much to tell. I'm always working. Something Borrowed is my life."

"Ever been married?" he asked.

"No. I was engaged once." *Damn, why did I open that can of worms?*

"What happened?"

Kelly swallowed hard. "He died."

He sat back, his eyebrows nearly touching his hairline over his wide eyes. "Bloody hell, I'm sorry."

That was everyone's response. They were sorry for her loss, sorry for her pain. What else could they say?

Still, she found it annoying, because it made her think about the past. About what could have been, and it still hurt. She wanted to be over it and never feel that sharp twinge in her chest again, but although it had faded, it still existed.

"It wasn't your fault. It happened eleven years ago."

"And you haven't been serious about anyone since?"

"No."

An awkward silence stretched between them. He probably thought she was some weird, obsessed woman forever pining for her lost love.

Rather than try to explain or assure him, she decided it was safer to change the subject. Kelly took a sip of wine before asking, "What about you? The tabloids said you were married once. What happened?"

"You've read enough Hollywood love stories in the tabloids. It's the same as the rest... We got together when we were first starting out in the business. My career took off and hers didn't. It put a strain on our marriage. Didn't make it past five years before she took me for half. Thank God we never had kids."

Hank spoke of it so matter of fact, but Kelly could tell the memory still stung by the tightening at the corners of his stormy gray eyes. "That really sucks."

He shrugged. "It's life. Sometimes you get lucky and other times, you come out with nothing."

She pulled her hand away from his and took another drink of her wine. Even though she'd lost Ray, she didn't feel as though she had nothing in her life. "I've been lucky in other aspects, if not in love. I've got a great business. Good friends. Chris."

"Chris, your lawyer?" he asked.

"Yeah, and best friend. We've known each other since we were thirteen."

He quirked one eyebrow. "Never dated?"

"Not once. It's always been platonic." *At least, it used to be.*

"No such thing."

Her eyes narrowed in irritation. "Excuse me?"

"I'm just saying that men and women cannot be friends. Eventually, someone is going to confess their feelings and when the other person rejects them, it will ruin the illusion of friendship forever."

"The illusion of...good God, you're a pessimist."

Hank clucked his tongue, his expression scolding. "I'm a realist. Either you are holding a candle for him or he's got a big old shine for you. Either way, you're fooked."

She bit her lip to keep from laughing at the way he said *fucked*. It almost completely dissolved her annoyance with him, it was that cute.

Of course, almost didn't count. Especially when she was already sensitive where Chris was concerned. "We aren't. Chris was best friends with my fiancée, Ray. Believe me, he feels nothing more than brotherly toward me."

Hank leaned forward, bringing his face closer to hers. "It's you then, is it? You got a thing for your fancy lawyer friend?"

She moved a little closer, teasing him. "Nope."

Hank cocked his head to the side and scoffed. "I don't believe it, but there's one true test to be sure."

"And what's that?"

"Get naked in front of each other."

Kelly nearly blew wine out of her nose. "What?"

"Ye heard me. Parade around him in nothing but your birthday suit. If he doesn't jump your bones he's either not interested or gay. Same goes for you."

Kelly coughed, trying to disguise her laughter. "You're a terrible man."

"Not what you'd be saying if you stripped for *me*, love."

Kelly's cheeks flushed with embarrassment and she finished the rest of her wine with an unladylike gulp. She set her glass on the bar with a clink and stood. "I should probably get home."

"I was just teasing you, darling." He caught her wrist in his big warm hand, stroking the inside with his thumb. "I promise to behave if you stay."

Kelly pulled from his grasp and dipped down to give him a peck on the cheek. "It's almost ten and I have to be at the office early."

"You sure I can't change your mind?"

For a grown man, his pout was rather adorable, and she caught her bottom lip between her teeth so she wouldn't smile. His ego was far too healthy as it was.

"Not tonight, Hank, but thank you. I had fun."

Hank groaned. "Oi, she said *fun*. I'm doomed."

She placed her hands on her hips with a huff. "I could have said you were boring and I never want to see you again."

"Do you want to see me again?" His eyes bored into hers with a seriousness that made her shift her feet.

Hank was nice and funny. They could go out for dinner and drinks without breaking her protocol, especially since the mere touch of his hand didn't send her into an excited state of lust.

"Yes, I think I would."

His self-satisfied grin took up his whole face. "Well, then there is that, I suppose."

"Goodnight," she said, a hint of laughter in her voice.

He stood up next to her, and even though he had tipped the bartender earlier, he put another bill on the bar. "I'll walk you to your car. There could be fiends about."

"In Sweetheart? Please."

"All the same, I'll see you out."

Kelly picked her phone up off the bar. He placed his hand on the small of her back, gently leading her outside and she smiled. She'd had a good time, and Hank *was* charming. She didn't remember much about her first date with Ray except his hands were sweaty and she'd been so nervous she kept having to leave the movie theater to pee.

So far, her grown-up dating experience had been a dud. At least she liked Hank.

*Maybe I should just say to hell with the rules for once.*

But as she paused just inside her car door, looking up at his handsome face shadowed in the street lights, the words, "Come home with me," froze in her throat.

"I'll see you Friday, Hank."

"Unless I see you before that." He winked at her as he backed up and made his way one row down to a silver Porsche.

Kelly climbed into the driver's seat and shut the door. Well, that had been a bust. Why the heck couldn't she do casual sex? She's seen it done hundreds of times in movies and television. Most men didn't turn down no strings attached romps in the sheets, so the risk for rejection was low.

She turned the key in the ignition, realizing that it was probably a good thing she didn't suggest they get it on. Hank was going to be her client for several more weeks. It would be awful to have a casual fling and either one or both be disappointed in the other's performance. Hank was probably a sex god who knew every move and position to make a woman come, while Kelly…

Well, her experiences had all been with Ray for about three months before he deployed. They'd had sex a couple times while he was on leave, but other than that, she was not exactly a rock star in the bedroom.

Besides, she wanted a serious relationship, right? Not some love-her-and-leave-her fling with an actor.

*I haven't lived at all since I was twenty years old. I have buried myself in work for eleven years. It's time that I get a life.*

She needed to get some experience and take life by the balls. And maybe, by the time the summer was over, she'd give Hank what he wanted.

Her phone beeped, and she swiped her thumb over the screen. Chris had finally texted her back.

*Hey, sorry, I just got home. Heading to bed.*

Kelly threw her car into reverse and revved out of the parking spot with a vengeance. Oh no he wasn't. They were going to have this out right now.

# Chapter 10

Chris was sitting in his living room with his legs propped up on the coffee table, watching an episode of *NCIS*, when headlights flooded his living room.

"Shit." He ducked low, making his way over to the window. He looked out in time to watch Kelly climb out of her car, wearing her black swishy dress, as she liked to call it. Her hair was flowing around her shoulders in loose waves and she looked fit to kill as she stomped up his porch.

Beautiful, but completely homicidal.

She didn't even bother to knock, just barged right in.

"You!"

He sat back on the couch, pretending that he hadn't known she was there. "Me what?"

She stalked towards him, pointing a finger as she stood above him. "I have been texting and calling you for days! Why are you avoiding me?"

He crossed his arms over his chest. "I'm not. I told you, I had something to do tonight and then I came home to go to bed."

"You are a lying sack of potatoes! You have been giving me *sorry too busy to talk* texts all week. Now, what in the hell did I do to piss you off?"

He stood up with his hands in the air. "Whoa, take it easy. You didn't do anything."

"Really?" He winced at the sarcastic bite to that single word. "So, we aren't going to talk about what is bugging you?"

"There's nothing bugging me!"

"Fine, I'll be the adult then. Sunday morning, we were wrestling, and you got an erection."

Chris's jaw dropped. "What in the fu—"

"It's no big deal! It's a natural reaction to having my ass pressed up against your crotch, but that's all I thought it was! I didn't freak out or anything, so I have no idea why you're being such a weirdo about it."

What the hell was he supposed to say to her? She'd felt his cock hard against her and just brushed it off as though he got a boner all the time? As though he was a fourteen-year-old who couldn't control his body?

*Maybe she has a point? Why else did I get so turned on by Kelly unless I couldn't help myself?*

Still, she didn't have to just lay it out there like that.

"Okay, first of all, I am not avoiding you. Second, I appreciate that you are so accepting of my body's natural urges. And three, why are you wearing your fancy dress?"

"Well, if you'd had an actual conversation with me this week, you'd know I went for drinks with Hank."

That got his attention and not in a good way. His muscles tensed with irritation and his jaw tightened. "Hank, your client, Hank? The one you said you wouldn't meet up with outside the office because it would be inappropriate?"

"Yeah, so?" She crossed her arms and did her sassy-hip-popping stance. "I wanted to do something fun since you blew off Wicked Wednesday!"

"So, you decided to go out for drinks in your sexy, swishy dress with a client because I was busy?"

Her mouth fell open. "Did you just call my dress sexy?"

Chris didn't want to consider her face, at the carefully outlined eyes, the thick, sweeping lashes, or full, pouty mouth. He didn't want to notice that her chest was rising and falling rapidly, showing off her cleavage above the swoop of the dress's neckline.

"Isn't that what you call it?" he asked.

"No, I've called it my swishy dress, but never—"

"Does it matter, really? It's just a stupid dress!"

He hadn't meant it to come out quite so harsh, and by her stunned expression, she didn't know what to make of him.

"What is wrong with you?!"

Chris ran his hands through his hair with a wry laugh. "Seriously? You show up here talking about erections and throwing out accusations that I am avoiding you and there is something wrong with me?"

"Yes, because you always have your phone on you." Kelly's voice broke and he saw the sheen of tears in her hazel eyes before they spilled over, trailing down her cheeks. "And never, in our eighteen years of friendship, have you ever blown off Wicked Wednesday without being on death's door."

Chris's heart sank as Kelly cried, covering her mouth with her hand.

"Ah, dammit, Kel. Don't cry." He stepped into her and even though she struggled against him for a moment, he held on until she relaxed.

"I…just don't know…what I did."

All his defenses flew out the window as he felt Kelly tremble with sobs against him. "You didn't do anything. It was all on me."

She didn't say anything, just continued to soak his shirt with her tears, so he kept going, the semi-truth spilling out of him like a volcano.

"I'm sorry. You're right. I was avoiding you."

"Why?" she sniffled.

He rolled his eyes to the heavens. "I was embarrassed about the…erection."

"Really? That's it?"

He stared down into her upturned face and luminous eyes, lost in their mix of greens and yellows. "Yeah. I just didn't want you getting the wrong idea."

"What idea?"

"That I was a caveman who wanted to throw you over my shoulder and have my way with you."

She pulled away and slapped at his arm. "It's not like you said, 'Hey baby, wanna do it?!' when I felt it poking me—"

"Jesus, Kelly, *really*?"

"Sorry, I just meant that I didn't think anything about it until you started being weird. I mean, it's not like I've never had a physiological response to you I couldn't control."

Now, *that* was interesting. "Really?"

Kelly glared at him. "All right, seriously, you don't have to sound so intrigued. I'm only telling you this to make you feel better."

"I think you should tell me more," he teased, trying to lighten the mood.

"You're awful."

"Sorry. And by the way, if I was trying to get you into bed, I'd have a better pickup line than 'You wanna?'"

"I don't know. As the last few days have shown, you aren't as mature as I once believed."

"Cute."

"I know." Her arms loosely wrapped around his waist. "You know you can talk to me about anything right? You don't ever have to be embarrassed. No secrets."

Chris brushed back a strand of her dark hair, tucking it behind her left ear. "No secrets."

She laid her head on his chest with a sigh. "Good, because I don't know what I would do without you."

Chris's mind drifted to Maria and her advice to put some distance between him and Kelly. He opened his mouth to say something about it, but she spoke first.

"I love you."

He hugged her tight. "I know."

They stood there for a moment, silently embracing the other. He breathed her in, the familiar scent of Kelly washing over him. Making him feel at home.

"Wanna watch a movie now?" she asked.

Distance could wait until tomorrow. "Sure. Sounds like a plan."

# Chapter 11

Kelly stood in Rylie Templeton's kitchen, watching her friend and former employee as she poured batter into two round baking pans. Technically, the spacious kitchen belonged to her boyfriend, Dustin Kent, who had also worked at Something Borrowed for a time, but the two were practically living together anyway. The light wood cabinets were plentiful, and on the counter was a gorgeous standing mixer.

In the corner, lying on the brown swirled tile floor was Rylie's pit bull, Raider, his eyes closed in bliss as the warm sunshine came through the gigantic window and covered his back.

Rylie slid the pans into the double ovens and shut the doors. She spun around to face Kelly with a smile.

Rylie's brown eyes sparkled as she wiped her hands on the legs of her jeans. "You have some cake designs for me?"

Since she'd stopped being a bridesmaid at the end of last wedding season, Rylie had taken over making all the cakes for Something Borrowed. She was a genius when it came to the culinary arts and was using the money to open a gourmet bakery, hopefully in the newly renovated Buzzard Gulch.

"I do." Kelly pulled the pictures out of the folder in her hand and laid them across the counter. "So, we have a traditional Catholic wedding for three hundred people. She wants something like these."

The three and four tiered cakes were white with eye-catching colorful flowers. The cakes were all round, and Rylie picked up the one in the middle, her forehead wrinkling as she studied the picture.

"I think the four tiered will be the best for the number of guests." Rylie set the picture down and redid her long brown ponytail. "When do they want to come for a tasting?"

"We only have four weeks, so could you have something this weekend? And FYI, the bride loves chocolate and the groom likes fruit."

Rylie shook her head with a chuckle. "Nothing like springing things on me last minute."

"You're doing a tasting for the Walker wedding. I thought you could just add a few more samples and we'll schedule them close together."

"Yeah, that *would* have worked...except the Walker wedding is gluten free. I'll have to have separate samples for each couple."

Kelly cursed. "I didn't know that. How did I not know that?"

"Gotta keep up with the deets, boss woman," Rylie teased. "It will be fine. I already have the Walkers scheduled for ten, so if we do the...what are their names?"

"Flintstone."

Rylie rolled her eyes at the obviously fake name. "So, easily recognizable, and super VIP. Got it. We'll do them at four."

"Great. And Dustin's okay with you having them here?"

"He's good. My kitchen is too small to handle the amount of baking I do. Here, I can use the pool house kitchen and the double oven when I need them."

"I'm glad. I wouldn't want to step on any toes."

"Are you kidding? He likes when I take over his kitchen because I always leave him extras." Rylie walked over to the cupboard next to the sink and held up a large, black mug. "Do you want some coffee?"

"Sure, I'd love some." Kelly pulled the second folder out of her purse, and put it on the counter. "I need to schedule one more tasting, but I have to talk to Hank about it."

Rylie turned and gave her a quizzical look. "Who is Hank?"

"Hank Townsend, the actor. He's hired me to plan his sister's wedding."

Rylie's eyes widened. "Hank Townsend? Oh man! He is smoking hot! And when he talks..." Rylie trailed off as the back door opened and she whispered, "Swoon."

Raider jumped to his feet with a series of hair-raising barks. If Kelly didn't know what a lambchop he was, he would have been terrifying with his scarred face and flashing white teeth. Some teenagers had lit the poor dog on fire, and it had taken him months to heal his body as well as his trust, but Rylie had won him over, like she did everyone.

The dog's nails clacked against the floor as he raced into the adjoining room and Kelly heard Dustin Kent's voice as he greeted the dog.

"Hey, buddy! Are you excited to see me? Huh? You just want me to play with you. Where's your ball?"

Raider was a blur as he skidded back through the kitchen and out into the laundry room.

Dustin appeared in the archway of the kitchen and waved at Kelly. "Good morning, Kelly." Dustin was six feet tall and gorgeous. Rylie told her once she thought that he was a dead ringer for Tom Welling, with his black hair and blue eyes, and Kelly could see it.

And about ninety-five percent of the time, he was a nice guy.

"Morning."

Dustin made his way over to Rylie and wrapped his arms around her waist. He stared down at her so tenderly, that Kelly felt like a voyeur watching them.

"Got anything sweet for me?"

Rylie blushed. "Pervert."

Dustin dipped her over his arm without warning. Rylie let out a startled shriek, cut short by the blazing kiss Dustin planted on her lips. This time, Kelly did avert her eyes and stared at the door as Raider ran back in, a green tennis ball hanging out of the side of his mouth.

"So, who is making you swoon?" Dustin asked, sounding out of breath. Kelly figured it was safe to look at them again. Rylie's face was red, and her lips appeared a little swollen.

Was it weird that Kelly was jealous of the look in her eyes?

"What?" Rylie said.

"When I walked in I heard the word 'swoon.'"

Rylie seemed to collect herself as she pulled out of Dustin's arms and went back to pouring them coffee. "Oh, Kelly is working with Hank Townsend."

Dustin squatted down and took the ball from Raider's mouth. "The action star?"

"The very one," Kelly said.

"Who is he marrying?" He threw the tennis ball into the grand foyer of Dustin's mansion. Kelly had never had an official tour of all the rooms, but the high ceilings in the entryway and the sheer size of the outside told her that there had to be at least six rooms.

Raider ran in place for several beats before he shot off after the ball, making Dustin, Rylie, and Kelly laugh.

"Babe! If you play with him in the house, he is going to break something," Rylie said, setting a plate of powdered donuts on the counter.

Dustin just shrugged. "He's fine. Anything he breaks is on me."

Rylie rolled her eyes. Kelly knew that Dustin wanted Rylie to move in with him, but so far, she hadn't agreed. Kelly got the feeling that there was a lot not being said for Kelly's benefit.

"To answer your question, Hank isn't the one getting married. His younger sister is. He is just here to pay and plan it for her."

"Has he hit on you yet?" Dustin asked.

Rylie gasped. "Dustin!"

"What? Rumor is the guy is a ladies' man. Kelly's attractive, so it makes sense he would flirt with her."

"To answer your question, he has," Kelly said.

Dustin washed his hands and then came up behind Rylie. He slipped one arm around her waist and grabbed a donut with the other. "See? My question wasn't that crazy."

"I-told-you-so's are not sexy," Rylie grumbled.

The sound of crashing in the other room made Dustin laugh. "Are you sure? Because when you say it to me it makes me so hot, baby."

Rylie turned in his arms and started whacking him on the shoulder. "You are so gross." Her tone was heavy with mirth, and Dustin danced away from her with a wink.

"You think I'm adorable and you know it." Then he hollered, "Raider! What did you break? Now your mom is going to gloat that she was right!"

Dustin left the room, and Kelly watched Rylie, still smiling as she delivered Kelly's coffee to the counter in front of her. Kelly picked the mug up and walked over to steal a donut. "He makes you happy?"

"Very much." Rylie lifted her own cup of coffee to her mouth and sipped lightly. "It's funny, because after all the romance novels I've read, I never really expected to find anything like this. When we fight, I have this knot in the pit of my stomach, because the thought of losing him is so unbearable. I've never had that with anyone."

"I am so glad. You deserve the best."

Rylie shot her a pensive look. "So do you." She paused a moment, cradling her coffee cup between her hands as she stared at Kelly. "This Hank guy…is he going to be a problem?"

"How do you mean?" Kelly asked.

"Like a stalking, won't-take-no-for-an-answer, kind of problem."

Kelly knew Rylie's concern came from her own terrifying experience with an unhinged man she'd dated last year, so she didn't laugh.

"No, he's fine. Just likes a challenge."

"At least you have Christian watching your back at work."

Kelly involuntarily frowned at the mention of her friend. Even though they had talked and watched TV last night, it had been…off. Anytime she moved, he'd stiffened or gotten up to get something. As though he was afraid to touch her. Whatever was going on between them, they hadn't resolved it.

But as much as she adored Rylie, she wasn't going to talk about it. Besides, she had no idea what the problem was, so there was nothing to say. "Yep, I've got Chris."

# Chapter 12

Chris hadn't waited the full week to reach out to Rachel. In fact, he'd called her on Sunday and asked her out for Friday night. She'd sounded pretty excited, which made him less self-conscious about Maria's comments.

To his surprise, Kelly had cancelled on him for Wednesday, telling him she'd had to help Veronica with her first wedding. He'd almost dropped dinner off to them at the office but told himself that she'd done him a favor. He'd wanted to put some distance between them, and she'd done it for him.

But he missed her. Her smile, her laugh. Her body cuddled up next to his while they watched a movie.

God, he was a fucked-up mess.

He picked Rachel up from her place and took her to dinner at a Mexican-Korean restaurant. It had been her choice, not his; he wasn't a fan of overpriced, fusion food.

Dinner was fun, although he was still hungry. The tiny plate of tacos they'd served him had not been enough to sustain him. Rachel was two margaritas in, and getting flirty by the time he paid the check.

When they got outside, she asked, "What now?"

"I was thinking we could check out what's playing at the theater."

She stepped closer to him, her arms twining around his neck. "Or, we could go back to my apartment and see what's playing in your pants."

Chris grimaced. *Talk about stupid pick-up lines.*

Before he could respond, Rachel rose up on her tiptoes and kissed him. She pulled his head down to hers and opened her mouth against his lips. Chris was used to taking the lead, so he increased the pressure, putting his arms around her waist.

Nothing was happening. Not even a small stir of excitement. She was soft. She smelled good...but his cock was as limp as an old carrot.

"Get a room!" someone yelled as they drove by and it was the perfect excuse to end the kiss.

"Let's go," he said.

She took his hand as they walked to the car. He was attracted to Rachel, always had been. Maybe it was just because the kiss was so aggressive and out in the open that he hadn't been able to get into it. He was completely sober, while he knew Rachel was at least buzzed. He didn't feel right going to bed with her unless they were both in their right mind.

Meanwhile, Rachel was drawing little finger hearts on his upper thigh the whole way back to her place. She obviously had no issue with the two of them taking this to the next level.

Still, nothing.

After he parked, he climbed out and headed over to open the passenger door. Out of the corner of his eye, he saw something small and white run under a bush.

He helped Rachel out and let her take his hand again, but his attention was on the shrubbery.

"I am so glad we finally did this," she said.

Chris nodded distractedly. "Me too."

They passed by the bush and Chris heard a little squeak. He slowed his steps and stared down into the dense branches, searching for the source of the sound.

"What is it?" she asked.

"I heard something."

He released her hand. Then, Chris squatted down next to the bush and stuck his hand out to move some branches.

A tiny, white paw poked out and attacked his fingers with pinprick sharp claws.

Chris jerked his hand back with a startled laugh. "Hey, who is in there?" He turned to Rachel. "Do you mind getting the flashlight out of my glove box?"

"Ooookay."

Chris ignored her obvious irritation. He stuck his hand in again, and drew it back. This time, a tiny kitten popped its head out, its arms reaching for him. Its eyes were dilated, and its mouth was wide open, flashing its teeth playfully.

"Oh, you're tough." He grabbed ahold of the kitten and pulled him out of the bush. He felt the little body vibrate as he brought it against his chest.

The tiny cat was purring up a storm. He rubbed the kitten's ears and its eyes closed for a brief second.

Then, he wrapped his paws around Chris's hand and bit down gently, followed by a sweet lick on the back of his hand.

"You're a friendly little guy." Chris hadn't had a cat since he was a kid, but it seemed young. He could cradle the creature in one palm.

"What is it?" Rachel asked from behind his left shoulder.

"A kitten."

"Oh, great. I was afraid it was going to be a mouse." She took a step toward her apartment. "It's probably one of my neighbors'. They never fix their cats. They just let them outside and they keep breeding."

Chris frowned. "He's pretty little and skinny. I'm surprised he hasn't been a snack for something, being out here on his own."

"Well, he's obviously doing fine, so you should just put him back," Rachel said.

Chris thought about it. He could be someone's pet, but there was a busy road not too far and if Rachel was right and the people never fixed their pets, would anyone miss him if he disappeared?

"Which apartment has the cats?" he asked.

Rachel stared at him as though he'd lost his damn mind. "I don't know. I'm allergic, so I avoid them."

Chris could just start knocking on doors, but it was after nine. He didn't really feel like pissing a bunch of people off.

He started to put the little guy down, but suddenly, the kitten climbed up his chest. When the small head was right under his nose, the fur ball rubbed his face against Chris's cheek.

And that was it. He was owned.

"I'm going to keep him."

Rachel bit her lip. "But...I...I can't have him in my apartment."

"That's okay. We'll head home."

"What about coming in?"

"I should get this guy back to my place and feed him." He almost leaned over to kiss her cheek, but remembered her allergies. "I'll call you."

"Fine. Goodnight." He could tell she was miffed as she stomped to her door in her four-inch heels, but Chris was too caught up in the needle-sharp teeth currently eating the end of his finger. He had no idea what he needed for the little guy, but...

Kelly would.

He climbed into his truck and under the dome light, took a selfie of him and the kitten. Then he sent it to Kelly.

*I made a new friend. Help me?*

Seconds ticked by before she finally answered.

*Get your ass over here.*

Chris laughed and started the truck. One good thing about Kelly was no matter how mad she might be at him, she could never resist a critter in distress.

# Chapter 13

Kelly took several deep breaths, telling herself to calm the hell down. This was Chris, her dear friend and colleague. This wasn't the first time Chris had come over late at night when she was in her pjs. No reason to freak about it now.

So what if she'd had two sexy dreams about him in the last week? Who cares if she'd been so turned on when she'd woken up that she'd needed to alleviate the pressure with her battery-operated buddy? She couldn't control where her subconscious went and that was no reason to be weird around him.

She heard Chris come through the front door and pulled her gray sweater tighter around her body. She came around the corner to find him standing in her living room, holding a little ball of white and tabby fur in his big hand.

"Oh, my God, where did you find him?"

At the sound of her voice, the kitten's head popped up and he yawned adorably.

"Under a bush at an apartment complex."

"Outside? Poor pumpkin. He doesn't look older than six weeks." She walked closer to get a better look. The kitten's ears and back were brown striped while the rest of him was snowy white except…were those bald patches on his ears?

*Oh boy.*

"Bring him into the kitchen so I can get a better look at him."

Chris stroked the kitten's head and back as he passed her by, the scent of his cologne wrapping around her like a cozy blanket. She felt a little like a floating cartoon character following him with her nose in the air.

Dammit, she really needed to get a grip on herself!

She stepped closer to him, studying how small the kitten looked in Chris's big hands. Kelly didn't want to take the chance of meeting his pale blue eyes, especially less than a foot away. She scratched the kitten under his chin, turning his head this way and then the other, concentrating on searching for hairless spots and not on the fact that Chris's chest looked hot in the blue T-shirt he was wearing.

Once she got a good look at the little fuzzbutt, she noted the scaly bald spots and knew without a doubt she wasn't wrong.

"Hey Chris..."

"Yeah."

"Your new kitten has ringworm."

Chris turned into a statue right in front of her and she couldn't help meeting his wide eyes with amusement. "What is that?"

"It's a fungal infection. It won't hurt you or him, but it will need to be treated."

Chris held the kitten away from him a bit, and Kelly backed up quickly or his hands would have hit her right in the face. "What does it do?"

"It causes hair loss on cats and dogs, and little rings on people. It's really not a big deal."

Kelly couldn't help laughing at the horrified look on his face.

"Will you relax? We'll just get some anti-fungal cream, apply it several times a day and in a couple of weeks, it will be gone. Here, let me inspect him for more spots. I see at least three on his ears and head, but the paws and belly are also good places for the fungus to grow."

Chris handed the kitten off to her and immediately raced to the kitchen faucet. He turned the water on, lathering his hands up and scrubbing them furiously beneath the stream. She giggled as she turned the kitten over, looking for more spots. She was up to seven, as he was missing hair on both of his front paws.

He meowed in protest when she held up his tail to check his rear end...yep, a he.

"Looks like he's got about eight spots, including a suspicious one on his belly. We should take him into the vet tomorrow and get him some oral medicine along with the topical cream."

Chris shook his head. "I can't believe I tried to do something good, and I get bit in the ass."

"Geez, ringworm is really common in kittens. Pepper had it and look at him now." Upon hearing his name, Pepper padded into the room, his tail swishing in the air and meowing long and low.

"Is being a tubby, lazy fur ball a side effect?" Chris asked.

Kelly's gaze narrowed in irritation as he continued to watch the kitten in her hands as if it was a bomb about to go off. "I'm sorry, were you expecting pet ownership to be nothing but sunshine and rainbows? It's not. You think I like cleaning up Pepper's hair balls or scooping his litter box?"

The corner of Chris's mouth tilted up. "I'm guessing not."

"You would be correct. Now, take your fungus-riddled cat back."

"Nice," Chris said. He took the kitten from her and held it up to look him in the eye. "Did you hear the nasty things she said about you? You have my permission to hiss at her."

The kitten turned its head into Chris's thumb as he rubbed its ear.

Okay, so Kelly's heart melted a bit. She was a big old softy who loved those calendars featuring hot guys and baby animals. What warm-blooded, hetero woman didn't?

And Chris, in his semi-tight shirt and jeans, holding a one-pound kitten in his hands, was definitely calendar material.

Flashbacks of her X-rated dream swept across her mind and she silently cursed herself.

*I really need to stop thinking like that about Chris.*

Luckily, he was so focused on the kitten that he didn't notice her mini-meltdown.

"I don't suppose you have an extra litter box I could use and maybe some kitten food?" he asked.

"No, but I have some canned food and a cardboard soda flat. We could set him up with a little area in my bathroom while we run back to Walmart."

Chris groaned. "That's all the way on Motherlode Drive."

Kelly rolled her eyes. "Who are you? We used to hit up Walmart just because there was nothing else opened when we were in high school."

"Yeah, but we are adults now and I'm up past my bedtime."

She pointed at the kitten. "Look at that face. He needs things. Don't be an old poop."

He grumbled behind her as she went about readying the kitten's room. She wanted to be sure and keep the little guy separate from Pepper, so he didn't get ringworm again. The stuff was extremely contagious, if harmless, and she didn't want it in her bed.

Once she had the water, food, and makeshift litter box, she went into her spare bathroom to set up. She placed the food and water dishes closer to the sink while the litter box she set on the other side of the toilet. She bundled an old towel in the corner between the tub and the wall for the kitten to sleep on. Kelly stood up and surveyed her temporary home for the fur baby with a smile.

"All right, I'm ready for him," she called.

The first thing that struck her as Chris entered the bathroom was that the kitten was rolling over in Chris's hands, enjoying belly rubs. He hadn't been as relaxed with her, but some cats were just like that. They loved their owners from the first moment they met them and tolerated everyone else.

The second was she'd never thought of Chris as imposing, but stuck in such a small space with him, she realized that he nearly blocked the entire door. Not that they hadn't been in confined quarters before, but this was the first time she was fully aware of him. She was consciously thinking about the fact that if he wanted to, he could block her escape from the room. Maybe push that tight body up against hers and keep her in place until he was finished with her.

Her skin turned feverish and sweat broke out all over. "Here, let me squeeze by you and we'll see if he'll eat."

Kelly turned to the side and his hands, which were holding the kitten, brushed her chest. Heat rose up across her skin and her nipples hardened to pebbles.

She glanced at him to see if he'd noticed her reaction, but he was squatting with his back to her. The minute he set the kitten down, it raced to the food bowl. With both white paws planted in the middle of the kitten food, the kitten growled as he devoured the pâte and gravy.

Chris stood up, and waved his hand toward the door. "Come on, let's get out of here, and get cleaned up."

She couldn't get out of the claustrophobic space fast enough. They walked out of the room into the hallway and Kelly reached for the door at the same time he did. She dropped her hand away like his skin burned her and nervously stepped back as he shut the door.

"Are you okay?" he asked.

"Yeah, why?"

"Cause you've been jumpy since I got here."

Drat, the last thing she wanted to do was draw attention to the face that *something* was different between them, even if it was all on *her* side.

"Sure, I'm great. Just had one too many cups of coffee today."

She could tell by the arch of his eyebrows that he didn't believe her, but he seemed to let it go. "All right. If that's the truth, then we better get gone and back."

"First, scrub your hands and then get changed. You've got an extra shirt here still, right?"

"Yeah, bossy, I'm covered."

Kelly pursed her lips as her gaze traveled from his head to his feet involuntarily. "Might not be a bad idea to take a shower. Make sure you get every inch he may have touched. I'll even throw your clothes in to wash, if you want."

Hank's suggestion that the two of them get naked in front of each other came unbidden to her mind as Chris shrugged. "Sure. I'll be quick. Want me to use yours since the kitten is down here?"

She tried to remember if she'd left anything embarrassing like bras or underwear lying about.

*Chris has seen my room a complete mess, so why am I stressing about underwear?*

"That's fine," she said.

As Chris disappeared up the stairs, Kelly's eyes gravitated to his butt. She couldn't see much, since his jeans were loose fitting, but she could imagine it was as tight and firm as the rest of him.

Once he was out of sight, she groaned. It was about time that she admitted that she had the hots for Chris. Fighting it wasn't working, so she might as well embrace it.

What that meant, she had no idea yet.

Her phone chirped and it was Hank.

*Hey Gorgeous. Would you like to
meet me for dinner tomorrow?*

*I don't think that's a good idea.*

*You can bring Julia's giant folder if it will
make you feel better. Then you can pretend
it's a work dinner while I entertain you with
tales of our future with five children.*

Kelly smiled, her brain protesting as her heart begged her to let loose for once.

*Fine, I will meet you for dinner.*

*Fantastic. Is it pushing my luck if I tell you I haven't been able to stop thinking about wanting to kiss you?*

Kelly's stomach dropped to her knees. She knew Hank was a flirt, but what if he tried to kiss her? She hadn't kissed anyone in eleven years and he was a damn Lothario! What if she sucked?

The sound of the shower turning on upstairs distracted her from her panic attack for a half a second before it all rushed back over her. She needed to start off slow. Find someone comfortable to practice on so when Hank laid one on her she wasn't completely hopeless.

Chris belting the lyrics to "More Than a Feeling" traveled through the flooring and Kelly got an idea. With Chris and her having this weird vibe between them, things had been tense. But, if they kissed and proved there was nothing more than friendship between them, it would kill two birds with one stone.

Now, she just had to figure out how to get Chris to kiss her.

# Chapter 14

Chris pushed the cart through Walmart with Kelly by his side, putting his foot up on the back of it and gliding forward across the white linoleum squares. The fluorescent lights above them were like spotlights.

"Nice, very mature," she said.

"What? You said to treat this trip like we're back in high school."

"I just wanted you to go to the store with me, not act like a nerd bomber riding carts up and down the aisle."

Chris stopped in front of the cat food and turned to her with a wicked smile. "Wanna climb into the basket and give them a real show?"

"Are you crazy? I'm not climbing in there and letting you push me around. That's how I broke my arm junior year."

"Hey, it wasn't my fault! Ray was driving."

Their banter faded at the mention of Ray's name, and Chris wished that it didn't still hurt. Especially the last few weeks, when he'd had such conflicting emotions where Kelly was concerned, the thought of Ray on top of that had made his guilt palpable.

It had never been awkward to talk about Ray before, but the silence was strained now.

*Because Ray was always the buffer between me and her, and then it was her grief and work.*

Now there was nothing to blind him to the fact that he wanted Kelly.

So freaking bad.

Kelly cleared her throat and grabbed a couple of cans of cat food off the shelf. "Here's some wet food, which you can wean him off if you hate the smell." She set the food in the cat and walked across the aisle to the other ceiling high metal shelves. "I'll grab a bag of kitten food too."

"I can get it," he said.

"Please, it's like 8 pounds. I can handle it"

He intercepted her, grabbing the yellow bag with a triumphant whoop, trying to regain the carefree interactions they'd had before he brought up Ray.

She rolled her eyes. "Congratulations, you got the food."

Chris set the bag into the basket. "Damn right I did. Now, I'll race you to the litter!"

He grabbed the cart and pushed off. He heard her laugh behind him and grinned. They could do this. Things didn't need to get weird.

She caught up with him, going neck and neck with the cart as they neared the rear wall where the cat litter was stacked on wire shelves.

Kelly got to the shelf first. She grabbed a plastic jug and held it over her head. "I am the master of the litter!"

Kelly did a little victory dance with the jug and Chris was struck dumb by how adorable she looked in her plaid pajama bottoms, gray sweater, and messy ponytail, doing the running man.

She stopped shaking her rear and frowned at him. "What? Do I have something on my face?"

He couldn't very well tell her he was caught up in her cuteness. "Nothing. I just miss this."

It wasn't a lie. He *did* miss this. Missed her.

Kelly set the jug of litter in the cart. Then, she held onto the side, a thoughtful expression on her face. "I have too. I am sorry things have been off between us lately." She turned her back to him, taking a litter pan off the shelf and kept talking. "Maybe it's because we're in our thirties and both single. I know we never made a pact or anything, but it's logical to start noticing your best friend, who also happens to be a good-looking guy, when your biological clock starts ticking."

"I don't know whether to focus on the fact you never thought I was attractive until now or that you're blaming it on your body telling you it's time to make babies."

She shot him an exasperated look. "Not what I said. I was just thinking that ever since I decided to date, there has been this tension between us. Haven't you noticed?"

*Yes, because I keep thinking about you naked.*

"Nope, just the same as always."

"Ugh, you are such a liar." She pulled a cat food dish and water dispenser off the shelf, tossing them in the cart.

"Why do you say that?" he asked.

Kelly kept heading down the aisle with him pushing the cart alongside her. "Um, maybe because you freaked out over a boner."

"Okay, that's not really something we need to discuss here," he said.

True there was no one on the aisle, but still…packages were never meant to be discussed in public.

"Fine, but you have to admit, the vibe between us has been freaky."

Chris turned the cart up another aisle, heading toward the front of the store. "I've had a lot going on at work and so have you. We're just in a funk."

Chris could see the lines of registers at the end of the aisle were several customers deep. Why was it anytime of day, Walmart was always busy?

"Hank thinks we need to strip down and stand in front of each other naked."

Chris almost hit a display of air fresheners, he stumbled so hard. "What?"

Kelly seemed oblivious to his initial shock. "He thinks we're harboring a secret lust for each other and the only way to know for sure is to display or goods and see if one of us pounces."

Chris didn't like that he was intrigued by Hank's suggestion, especially when he knew the guy just wanted to get into Kelly's pants. "And why are we discussing our friendship with a stranger?"

"It came up when we went for drinks last week. He asked if we'd ever dated and I said no, we were just friends, and he said that was bullshit. That women and men can't be friends because someone always wants the other. Then he told me the only way to prove that there are no lustful feelings was to get naked."

"Hank really said lustful feelings?"

"I'm paraphrasing, but yes."

They went to an open register in the self-checkout area, and Chris handed her items while she scanned them. "So, are you telling me that you peeked in on me while I was in your shower today and you found me wanting?"

"Of course not! I wouldn't spy on you!"

"Now I'm worried there may be a peephole in the bathroom somewhere."

She whacked him in the arm with the jug of litter. "Shut up! Someone is going to hear you and think I'm a pervert!"

"Relax. Pretty sure the woman who is supposed to be manning this area is asleep."

They both glanced over at the Walmart employee, who appeared to be nodding off where she stood. "Hurry and pay for your stuff so we can get out of here. I'm going to die of mortification."

He slowed down, loving the bright blush on her cheeks.

"You bastard."

"Let's see…" He pulled his wallet from his back pocket and removed his debit card. Staring at the screen as though befuddled, he tapped the card on his bottom lip. "Now, how do I pay?"

"I am going to kill you."

"Why so serious?" he asked, tilting his head to the side as he looked at her.

She threw up her hands and stomped outside, leaving him alone in front of a talking machine. He'd thought they were just playing, but obviously, he'd missed something major.

He finished his transaction and pushed the cart outside, scanning the area for Kelly. He finally spotted her next to his car, pacing.

Chris pushed the cart up alongside the truck, scowling at her. "Hey, what was that? I was only kidding about the peephole."

"Yeah, I know, it's one big joke to you," she said sarcastically.

"What's one big joke?"

"Can you please open the truck? I'm cold."

Chris had no idea how, since it was still seventy degrees outside. He unlocked his truck and she climbed inside. He loaded up the groceries, completely bewildered by her anger. How had they gone from laughing and playing around to her sitting silently in the front seat?

Chris climbed into the passenger seat and just sat there, watching her as she stared out the passenger window.

"All right, are you going to explain to me what in the hell I did to make you lose your shit?"

"Nothing," she mumbled.

"You just stomped out of Walmart like they were out of a blue light special. So, I'll ask again…why did you run out like that?"

She turned away from the window and met his gaze head on in the dome light.

"Fine. I don't think what's going on with us is a joke."

"What's going on with us?"

Kelly's hands fluttered between them. "The sexual tension. It's obviously something that isn't going away, and I think we should test the theory."

Chris was confused by the sudden shift from sullen to excited. "What theory?"

"The friendship theory."

His jaw flopped open. "You want to get naked with me?"

"No, of course not. Nothing so extreme."

"Then what…"

"I think you should kiss me."

# Chapter 15

Kelly hadn't meant to just blurt it out like that, but there was no calling the words back now. She'd gone there. She'd asked Chris to kiss her, and he appeared petrified by the suggestion.

How freaking humiliating.

She hadn't liked him making fun of her or teasing her about spying on him when he was naked. Even though she'd been a little tempted to check him out…she would never actually walk in on him. She knew he was joking, but it had hit too close to home for her comfort.

Still, that was no excuse to throw that at him like that. She'd been trying to feel him out, but that had escalated quickly.

The fact that he had said nothing for nearly thirty seconds worried her that she may have given him a mini-stroke. Ouch.

"Is it really so horrifying?"

"Maybe not horrifying, but you asking me, your best friend of eighteen years, to kiss you out of the blue? Little bit surprising."

She gripped her hands in her lap nervously. "Wow. I was just thinking that the two of us have been on edge with each other, and maybe we just need to…satisfy our curiosity."

He went quiet again and Kelly was frankly relieved that he hadn't denied their chemistry. Otherwise, she'd have probably jumped out of the car and walked home.

"What are you curious about? Whether I kiss like a thirsty camel? I assure you, I don't."

"Why would I want to kiss you if you did?" He didn't seem to have an answer for her and she snapped, "Are you really that scared to kiss me?"

"I'm not scared! I just don't want to make it weird."

She couldn't believe they were sitting in the Walmart parking lot, arguing about whether they should kiss. "Oh, you mean like avoiding me and acting as though I'm this hideous creature you've never thought about kissing?"

"Of course, I've thought about kissing you, Kel. I'm a guy and you're a beautiful woman. But then I tell myself what a bad idea it would be."

She wanted to press him on why exactly it would be bad, but was afraid of the answer. That even though he was attracted to her and loved her like a friend, she wasn't what he was looking for.

And that bothered her more than she could say.

"Look, Chris...I have not been out with anyone except a sue-happy man with an anger management problem. And there is a very experienced guy who hasn't been shy about wanting to take me out, and I'm afraid I'll embarrass myself if he kisses me."

Chris's expression clouded over. "Are you talking about Hank?"

"Yes, I am talking about Hank!"

"I thought you weren't going to do anything with him because he is a client?"

"Well, I changed my mind! He's attractive and charming and I deserve to have a little fun!"

"Then what in the hell do you want to kiss me for?"

"What if I'm a bad kisser? It's been so long, I might have forgotten."

Chris groaned. "You're not going to be a bad kisser, Kel."

"How do you know? I am out of practice and what if I forget to swallow my spit and I drool all over him?"

"So, you want to use me to practice on and drool all over me?" There was no real bite to his words and hope bloomed in her chest. Was he warming to the idea?

Kelly placed her hand on his bicep. "You're my friend. I know at least if I'm bad, you'll tell me the truth."

For a moment, she thought he was going to lean across the seat and do it. His body stiffened, and he shifted ever so slightly towards her, his gaze narrowing.

Instead, he turned away from her and started the truck. Her hand fell away from his arm, the rejection like a slap across the face. When he backed out of the parking space, Kelly sank against her door, tears pricking her gaze. She'd been an idiot to ask. It wasn't fair to Chris and it was a stupid idea anyway.

The drive back to her place was silent, until Chris flipped on the radio. Alternative rock filled the empty space, and Kelly discreetly wiped at her eyes.

"Are you crying?"

"No," she said, her voice thick with emotion.

"Ah, hell."

Chris jerked the truck onto the side of Bucks Bar Road, right above the drop down to the Cosumnes River below. When the truck stopped on the dirt, he shoved it into park.

"What are you doing?" she cried.

Chris shifted in his seat until he was turned to face her, his expression a mix of annoyance and concern. "I'm not going to sit here and listen to you cry for twenty minutes."

His tone sent fissions of fury across her skin and she reached for the door handle. "Then I'll walk."

Chris grabbed her arm gently but firmly, and didn't let go when she tried to pull away.

"You're being a real jerk, you know that?"

"I'm trying to apologize, if you'll just let me," he said.

"Not interested."

His face snapped into a scowl. "Well, too bad, because you're not walking on this road at night, so you're stuck with me."

She crossed her arms mutinously across her chest and waited.

"You threw me for a loop, is all. Not because I never wanted to kiss you and see what it would be like. I have, several times over the years. But not like this. Not to be used as practice for another guy you *really* want to kiss."

*I don't know if I'd say I* really *want to kiss him.*

Chris's hand cupped her chin, and the dome light came on. She blinked her eyes as they adjusted to the light and then met Chris's intense gaze.

"Kissing you now would be cheap and meaningless. If or when we kiss, I want it to be me you're thinking about."

Kelly's heart was hammering so fast she couldn't keep count of the beats, and her breathing became shallow and rapid. That sounded romantic. Had he meant it that way?

And why did his honest, heartfelt admission make her want to close the distance between them?

His hand, which had been so warm against the skin of her jaw, fell away and he smiled. "I'm sorry if I came off as a jerk."

She swallowed hard, her mouth dryer than her childhood sandbox.

"It's okay. I get it."

"Do you?"

No, she didn't. She thought Chris had refused to kiss her because she didn't really want to kiss him.

Except, she was pretty sure she did want to kiss him, because she was freaking disappointed that he was denying her again.

But instead of pushing the issue, she nodded. "Of course. Let's get back to the kitten."

He flipped off the dome light and pulled back onto the road. Kelly stopped crying, instead staring at the passing dark outlines of the pine trees.

Chris had refused to kiss her because he didn't think she wanted him.

*Or, Chris was just being nice because he doesn't want to hurt my feelings. I was practically sexually harassing him, which would have been really bad if we weren't friends.*

She just needed to forget all this craziness and go back to thinking of Chris as her friend. No muscles under tight T-shirts. His eyes weren't even that pretty and he didn't smell *that* great.

She could do this.

# Chapter 16

On Friday, Kelly sat at her desk across from Veronica, a stack of papers to her right. She was reading over the final menu for the Valdez wedding, which included a chicken and beef dish, spicy rice, beans, and a signature drink of sangria that they were calling a "Telejandro Forever."

Kelly smiled as she set aside the menu for the Valdez wedding and met Veronica's nervous gaze across the desk.

"I've got to say, V, I am really impressed with the effort you've put into this wedding. In just two weeks, you have handled everything to the bride and groom's satisfaction, and my own."

Veronica beamed at her as she gathered up her binders and notebooks. "Thanks, Kelly. I appreciate you giving me this chance."

"You cousin told my new assistant when she was leaving the other day that you were made for this kind of thing."

"I just want her to have the perfect day. By the way, how is Samantha working out?"

Samantha was Kelly's new assistant. Kelly had hired her on the spot when she'd come in for her interview because the girl had already finished college with a degree in hospitality and was looking for an entry level position in order to learn about wedding planning. Veronica had been training her in between her bridesmaid's duties. It had been a pretty smooth transition, but with a place like Something Borrowed, Kelly was used to the high turnovers. Most women only stayed the summer or a year tops.

And with Samantha's plans to eventually start her own business elsewhere, Kelly figured hiring her bought her another year.

"She's good. Gone home for the day, which is what the two of us should do now."

"Amen to that. Are you seeing Hank tonight?" Veronica asked.

Kelly shook her head. "Hank needed to go back to LA for a top-secret audition, and won't be back until next week. But that reminds me, can you still come by tomorrow and help me slap stickers on the little mason jars for the Townsend wedding?"

"Sure, that's fine. How many are we doing?"

"Three hundred and ten to be safe."

Veronica shook her head. "Aren't they loaded? Why can't they just buy cute wedding favors like other rich people?"

"No idea, but it isn't a question we'll be asking them," Kelly warned.

"I know, I know. Hey, what is going on with you two? I know the rule is no fraternizing, but I've seen the way he looks at you when you aren't paying attention and I think he likes you for real."

Kelly didn't want to hear that Hank might have real feelings for her. She liked his company, the fun and flirty banter, but even if Hank was interested in more, she wasn't.

"Hank is fun, and I enjoy his company, but we live very different lives. Even if I was willing to bend and break the rules, I don't see much of a future there."

Veronica shot her a pointed look. "You know, boss, sometimes you have to live in the now and stop thinking about anything further than that. Tomorrow isn't promised, after all."

"Thank you, Facebook Meme."

Veronica laughed. "All right, I am out of here before you take back every nice thing you just said."

"I would never take back an honest opinion."

Kelly smiled as Veronica escaped from her office, realizing that there really wasn't anything to rush home for, except to feed Pepper. No Friday plans except a couch with her name on it.

Considering a week ago she'd had a potential date and her best friend tell her that he wanted the first time they kissed to be special, it was kind of a letdown. Not that she'd gotten to experience the actual date. Hank had cancelled their dinner plans last weekend for an emergency with his agent, but he'd texted her constantly, even called her a couple of times at night. She really liked him, but she wasn't lying when she said she couldn't see a future there.

Of course, Veronica had a point about seizing the moment.

Kelly noticed the green message light flashing in the corner of her phone. She picked up her phone from the desk and slid her thumb over the screen. A message from Chris was waiting for her, and when she clicked on it, it was a picture of Chris lying back on his couch. On his chest was Fungi, pronounced FUN-GUY by Chris, curled in a ball with a smile on his furry face with a text attached.

*He hasn't left me alone since I got home.*

Kelly thought it was funny how in love Chris had become in so short a time. Despite the kitten's fungal infection, Chris never skipped a chance to hold his new pet.

*You don't look too unhappy about it.*

She slipped her phone into her purse, and set her computer bag on her desk. She slid her laptop inside and shut off the light to her office as she left the room. It was past eight according to the lobby clock, and she was so ready for something easy for dinner and bed.

She didn't really want to cook, but the only alternative was Subway or takeout from Shotgun, and she'd had both multiple times this week. She just wanted to go home, get into her jammies and relax.

When she arrived at her house fifteen minutes later, she went upstairs first to slip into her pjs and out of her silk camisole and pencil skirt. She trotted down the stairs and back to the kitchen in her tuxedo cat pajama bottoms and a black tank top.

Now, for food.

As Kelly searched, she found the motherlode in her cupboard. A package of Kraft Mac and Cheese. She was thrilled to check the fridge and find milk and butter inside.

Perfect dinner. Easy and delicious.

While her water boiled, she fed Pepper, who was winding his way around her legs dangerously. Then, she washed and cut up an apple, so she could at least pretend she was trying to eat healthy. She chewed on the sweet crunchy fruit as she poured the noodles in. Her phone beeped and she picked it up with her free hand, as the other popped another piece of apple in her mouth.

It was a message from Hank.

*Hello, Beautiful. What are you doing tonight?*

*Making mac and cheese and going to bed. I am so tired, everything looks like a pillow, including my kitchen counter.*

*LOL*

Kelly smiled in response, although she wasn't exaggerating. She hadn't realized how tired she was until she'd walked through the door.

She drained the pasta into a colander and carried it back over to the pot, dripping water across her tile floor. She'd get to it in a minute. She didn't like to clean and prepare food at the same time.

Once she'd stirred in everything, she poured a healthy portion into a bowl. She set her pot in the sink, then pulled the bottle of ketchup from the fridge and grabbed a spoon from the drawer.

She'd eat, watch an episode of something on Hulu, and then head to bed. Who cared if it wasn't very exciting?

Suddenly, her foot hit something slick on the floor and in a flash, she remembered the pasta water she'd meant to wipe up. Without thinking, she reached out to keep herself from falling.

The good news was, she didn't fall. The bad was that her arm was lying across the still hot burner as the oven had been the closest thing to catch herself on.

"Ow!" She screamed, jerking her arm off and turning it over to examine the damage. She stared down at the thick lines that spanned her inner wrist and forearm. It was like a brand across her skin, and although the initial hurt was gone, a terrible throb beat right where the burn was.

She slowly eased over to the sink. Kelly turned the faucet to cold water and as the stream fell across the burn, a painful breath hissed out through her teeth. The cold water soothed the sting for several minutes, until the frigid water itself became unbearable. Finally, she shut off the water and walked carefully across the floor, so she could get to the burn cream in her first aid kit in the kitchen cupboard.

She found it easily and carried it into her spare bathroom. Kelly sat down on the toilet and stared down at the angry blisters and peeling skin that had risen up on her arm. She'd never had a burn this bad; was it second degree? She had no idea what the criteria was, so she'd have to Google it.

After she put some of the burn cream on, she figured it would be fine. She'd get her dinner and go back to her originally scheduled program.

She walked back down the hallway and found Pepper on the counter, licking her mac and cheese greedily. He opened his mouth wide and an orange cheesy noodle disappeared down his throat.

"Pepper!" she yelled.

He threw his head up and when she took a step toward him, he jumped off the counter and sauntered out of the room, as though she was no real threat.

Kelly's eyes filled with tears as her arm began to throb.

Her dinner was ruined, her arm hurt like a son of a gun, and her plans of relaxing on the couch with a little binge-watching fun were destroyed.

She grabbed her phone off the counter and went to the couch. There was another message from Hank, but she ignored it and scrolled down. She could call her mom and dad, but since they lived in Arizona, alerting them to a possible medical emergency would just cause them undue worry.

Kelly spun through her contacts and pressed call when she found Chris's name.

He picked up on the second ring.

"Hey."

"Hi. So, I just burned the crap out of my arm."

"What do you mean?"

"I mean that I slipped in the kitchen and instead of just falling on my ass, I grabbed onto the top of the oven, and my arm landed across the piping hot burner."

She could hear Chris's breath hiss out. "Jesus, Kelly, how bad is it?"

"I really hurts. It didn't at first, but now it is throbbing, and the skin is peeling."

"I'm on my way over."

"Wait, I haven't even told you the worst part."

"What is the worst part?"

Kelly's sniffle ended in a wail. "I was making mac and cheese and left it alone to put burn cream on my arm and Pepper ate it."

Chris coughed, and she had a feeling he was laughing. "What a dick."

"Right?"

"So, you're telling me you're hungry too."

"Uh huh."

"I'll take you for food on the way to the ER."

Kelly's stomach twisted. She hated hospitals. "The ER? Why do I need to do that?"

"Because it sounds like you have a possible second or third degree burn and those get infected really easy. It needs to be seen."

She sighed, too tired, hungry, and hurt to argue. "Fine."

"Take some pain meds and hang tight. I will be there soon."

# Chapter 17

"Well, that's going to be an awesome bill," Kelly said as she walked ahead of him into her house.

He sighed heavily. "You know, that is the fourth time you've said that in three hours."

"I'm sorry, but I was feeling much better after the two ibuprofen I took kicked in. I could have waited until tomorrow when my doctor opened up."

She flipped on the living room lights and when Pepper opened his eyes slightly, she gave him the finger. "You're on my list, kitty cat. No pounce treats for you this week."

Pepper yawned widely and stood up, kneading the couch cushion. Chris would have almost said the cat was giving her bedroom eyes.

"Don't you try to seduce me with cuteness. You ate my mac and cheese. In some houses, that is punishable by kicking your butt outside to fend for yourself."

Chris shut the door behind him and locked it, holding onto his patience by a thread. "Stop threatening the cat. First of all, they are empty threats because you would never put Pepper outside, and second, he cannot understand you."

"Oh, he understands that I am pissed off for wasting the time and money at the ER when I'd have lived just popping pills and applying my own burn cream."

"Or, you could have woken up in excruciating pain with an infection. It's better to be safe than sorry."

"If it was your two-thousand-dollar bill, you might be thinking a little differently."

Chris made an irritated, guttural sound as he took the grocery bag of ice cream they'd bought on the way home and headed for the kitchen. "No, because you could have waited and ended up with a thirty-thousand-dollar bill when the infection spread to your liver or something, so how about you knock off the attitude?"

Kelly sat on the couch, her breath whooshing out of her lungs. "I'm sorry. I just feel so stupid about the whole thing. I knew that water was there, and I still slipped because I didn't want to stop my meal prep to wipe up the floor."

Chris came back into the room and handed her a bottle of water. "Here, stay hydrated. It was an accident. Could have happened to anyone."

She scoffed. "Come on. You never make mistakes like that. You're always perfect."

Chris sat next to her and put his arm around the back of the couch. "I'm perfect?"

Kelly turned her head and he watched her full lips dip into a frown. "Yeah. You were our high school valedictorian, you went off to kick ass at law school and I bet you already have your retirement account doubled by now."

"My account has doubled, but I set up your retirement too, so it's probably pretty close to mine. Plus, you got your business degree and make a fantastic living doing what you love. So how am I any better than you?"

Her voice was heavy with emotion as she responded, "I don't know. I just feel like I've been wasting time, and I realize that I'm going to be thirty-two in October. I spent my twenties buried in Something Borrowed, and I have nothing else. My friends have all moved away or are caught up in husbands and babies."

"You have the Buzzard Gulch project."

"That's true, but still, it's just another extension of Something Borrowed."

"And I don't see how you feeling as though you're wasting your life has to do with me being perfect?"

"Because at least you've tried things. I've never left Sweetheart, not even on vacation. You've been to Europe, Australia, and South America."

He'd been to more continents than that, but didn't want to make her feel bad by correcting her.

"You could have come on that senior trip with Ray and me."

She turned on the couch, so she was facing him. "Are you kidding me? My mother was already freaking out because she knew Ray and I were fooling around. She'd have never let me go because she was convinced I'd be kidnapped and murdered by a billionaire for sport."

Chris hoped she hadn't noticed his wince when she mentioned sex with Ray. Of course, he knew it had happened, but he didn't want to hear about it, even vaguely. "You realize that is the plot of *Hostel*, right?"

"Exactly. It was the last time I suggested we watch a horror movie together. She obsessed over it for months, and started researching human trafficking for hunting purposes."

Chris laughed. "Still, you could travel now."

"By myself? Color me pathetic."

"You have girlfriends."

"Who all left to go to college and explore the world."

"You're just determined to complain tonight, aren't you?"

Her cheeks turned bright red. "Sorry. I'm just…I want some excitement."

"And getting a second degree burn on your arm isn't thrilling?"

"No, dumbass, it is not."

Chris wrapped his arms around her and pulled her toward him, being careful of her gauze-wrapped arm. "You know, if you want to go somewhere, you could always ask me."

She relaxed against him with a laugh, her warm breath coming through his T-shirt and burning across the skin of his chest.

"You want to go with me to exotic locales?"

He kissed the top of her head. "Come on. I came back to Sweetheart because you wanted me to. There isn't much I wouldn't do for you."

Chris realized the implications of what he'd just said a moment before she lifted her head and met his gaze.

"There isn't?"

His heart rate kicked up a notch, creating a steady drumming in his ears. Before he could really think about the repercussions of what he was doing, he cupped her face in his hands.

"No."

Chris sensed her body leaning toward him and his hands slid down her neck and shoulders. They stopped on her biceps and rested there.

"I think that you are the smartest, funniest, and caring person on the planet, Kelly. You're something special."

Kelly closed her eyes and he met her halfway, their lips fusing together clumsily. Her hands buried in the front of his shirt and their mouths opened in unison, their tongues dancing with swift, tangled strokes. Chris had fantasized about kissing Kelly thousands of times, but doing it was so much better. Tasting her warm, sweet mouth on his. Touching her supple skin. Hearing the melodious sound of her heavy breathing between the brief breaking of their lips.

It was fucking paradise.

Kelly's arms came up and he felt them go around his shoulders right before she pulled away sharply, a strangled gasp escaping her mouth.

"Dammit!"

He realized she'd put her injured side of her wrist down on his shoulders and winced. "Are you okay?"

"Yeah, I just forgot for a moment."

He took her hand and brought it to his mouth, smiling gently. "I guess kissing me can be pretty distracting."

"Yeah, it really is." She adjusted her hand to slide her fingers through his. "Can we do it again? Please?"

The please was his undoing, and he cradled her cheek while keeping a hold of her hand. "We can definitely do that again."

# Chapter 18

Kelly softened her lips, following Chris's lead as they made out on her couch. She couldn't remember the last time she'd had a man's hand in hers, let alone pressing her onto her back. As he came over her, she was aware of every tight, sinewy piece of him against her front. Of the hard length of his cock through his blue jeans.

She spread her legs and placed her feet on the couch, bending her knees on either side of his hips. Her pajama pants were thin, and if she just lifted her hips, he'd be able to slide the shaft of his cock against the apex of her thighs. The thin material would do nothing to protect her, not that she needed or wanted it. For the first time in years, she felt alive. Rejuvenated. Horny as hell.

And it was all for a man who had seen her at her absolute worst and still called her special.

Chris reared back on his knees above her, breaking their kiss. Before she could beg him not to stop, he reached between them, and slipped his hand under her tank top, skimming his palm across her stomach. She stilled under him, watching him through half-closed eyes as he slowly made his way to her braless chest.

She didn't protest. Didn't tell him to stop, even when he lifted the tank up and over her head, tossing it across the room. She wondered what he was thinking as his gaze traveled from her navel up to her face, taking his sweet time getting there.

Then, with his blue eyes darker than she'd ever seen, he covered her breast with one hand and squeezed.

She moaned at the warm, firm grasp. God, it had been so long since she'd been touched and cared for and Chris…

She trusted him. Chris would never hurt her.

"Kelly, you are so fucking perfect. Everything about you."

He dropped his head and kissed the skin above her collarbone, the brush of his lips causing gooseflesh to erupt along the skin of her arms and stomach. She slid the fingers of her good hand through his hair and tugged, wanting his mouth back on hers.

He didn't give her what she was begging for, though. Instead, he stood up, standing over her with a heaving chest and tense, broad shoulders that lifted with every breath.

He was beautiful, and she wanted him. All of him.

"I...I'm sorry. I shouldn't have done that."

Wait, what? He was...he was stopping? *Now*?

She sat up, unconcerned with the fact that she was topless and her boobs had probably jiggled at the rapid motion. "Why shouldn't you have kissed me?"

Both his hands swept back through his hair, and he laughed, almost bitterly. "I have no fucking clue. I want you so bad, Kel, I don't know which end is up or down. All I do know is that I want to take you up those stairs and remove your pajama pants slow enough to give my mouth time to memorize the feel of your thighs beneath my lips. I want to kiss you until our lips are numb, and I want to bury myself inside you and feel the moment you come around me. But something is holding me back."

It was probably good that Chris was hesitating, trying to hold onto their platonic friendship.

Only his desires matched hers almost completely, and she really, really wanted him to follow through with it.

Kelly got up from the couch with ease, never breaking eye contact with him. When she stepped to him, his gaze devouring her, she wrapped her good arm around his neck.

"Don't hold back."

"Kel..."

"Shhh. Tomorrow, we can talk about why this can't happen again or how this was a mistake. But I am too tired tonight to lie about what I want right now."

Chris tenderly brushed her hair back from her face, his expression searching. "What do you want, Kelly?"

Kelly pressed her body flush against his. "I want you, Chris. I've wanted you for weeks, but had no idea how to ask for it. I'm asking now." She brushed her lips lightly against his. "Take me to bed."

Chris gripped her hips in his hands and brought her against him roughly. His mouth claimed hers and she lost herself in him. She could sense him moving them, driving her backwards. She was too caught up in his kiss to care when they bumped her side table and her crystal lamp shattered against the wood floor.

"Sorry about that," he murmured against her mouth.

Kelly's hands were under his shirt, trailing her fingers over the muscles of his back.

It wasn't until her legs hit the back of a mattress before she realized he'd maneuvered her into her spare bedroom. She fell back on the bed and watched as he stripped off his shirt. His cut torso was all angles and planes. Seeing Chris naked did not bring out feelings of indifference.

It made her hungry.

Kelly waited for Chris to continue undressing, leaning back on her hands, which caused her breasts to jut forward proudly. Instead, he stood with his hands on the snap of his jeans, staring at her chest.

"Aren't you going to take those off?" she asked.

"I was, but I got distracted."

She came up on her knees and grabbed him by his belt, pulling him to her. "Let's get you back on track then. This belt gets unbuckled. Then, I unbutton your jeans."

Chris let her do everything she described and more. When it came time to slide his jeans and underwear down, she lost her boldness for a moment, staring at the length of him through his underwear.

When Chris cradled the back of her neck, she met his tender gaze.

"You don't have to put on a show. I want you. Be real with me."

Her stomach knotted a bit as she remembered the summer with Ray after high school. Figuring out what he liked and what made him excited. The biggest thing for him had been when she did whatever he asked. He'd always had control in their sex life and she'd never thought of it until now. Now, here was Chris, letting her do what she wanted to him, telling her to be real and it was hot.

Smoking hot.

She pushed his pants and underwear down. His cock burst out of the elastic, and bobbed long and thick in her face. Without any cues from Chris, she wrapped her hand around him and lowered her mouth to his tip. Her tongue came out, tracing the head of him. Her lips followed, swallowing him up and sliding down until he touched the back of her throat.

"God, Kel."

She took his groan as consent as she played with him, testing what she liked. He tasted slightly salty and at first, she moved her mouth up and down him slowly, listening to every hitch of his breath. Kelly liked the sounds Chris made when she did something he enjoyed, and she wanted to keep it up.

"Fuck, stop. Stop."

She let her hand fall before she pulled her mouth away, releasing him with a wet pop. She sat back on her heels, smiling up at him.

"You were going to blow, huh?"

He laughed harshly. "Yeah, I was. And I'm not ready for this to be over."

The way he said it, so earnestly, made her skin tingle. He untied her pajama bottoms and pulled them down, leaving her only in her white and blue polka dot briefs.

"If I'd known this was going to happen, I would have worn something sexier," she said.

"You'd be sexy in anything."

He hooked the edges of her panties and pulled them down her legs, tossing them off to the side. Now, as naked as he was, she had the overwhelming urge to cover up, feeling too exposed and sprawled against the bed.

She caught him watching her, his eyes scanning her body earnestly, and she stilled. No one had ever looked at her like that.

He stepped out of his jeans and underwear, which had gathered around his ankles, then put one knee on the bed. Lifting her leg up over his shoulder, he traced the core of her with his finger until he reached the top where her clit lay nestled, begging for his touch.

He met her gaze over her naked, heaving body and smiled.

Then dipped his head between her legs and she stopped breathing. Licks of fire spread down her legs and up, curling in her belly as he stroked her with his tongue and fingers. Kelly's breath came out in a whoosh as he crooked one digit inside her and swept it over her g-spot.

"Holy…oh…my…shit."

Chris chuckled against her, his hot breath burning her flesh as his tongue pressed into her clit, massaging the bud rapidly. It was so fast, she barely had time to process one sensation to the next. All she knew was that pressure was building inside her and she was getting close.

She lifted her head to look down at his golden one and her whole body trembled. She couldn't see what he was doing, and then he looked up at her, his mouth covering her clit, his eyes glittering in the dark.

And he sucked so hard her back bowed. Her head fell against the bed and her eyes closed as the orgasm overwhelmed her, making her a tight, quivering mess as she came down. Her limbs turned into liquid until she could no longer hold herself up, and she sank into the mattress with a sigh.

She felt him move up next to her as she caught her breath, the heat of his skin pressing against her side, his hand trailing up her stomach, chest, until he was cradling her face.

"If you want me to stop, I will."

She opened her eyes and met his in the glow of the light coming from the doorway. She could see the desperation there, and knew he was silently begging her not to say no.

She didn't want to do that.

Kelly placed her hand on his cheek and lifted her head to kiss him. With her lips pressed against his, she whispered, "Please, don't stop."

# Chapter 19

Chris pressed his mouth down on hers as he swung his legs back between Kelly's shapely thighs. This night was like a dream, one he didn't want to wake up from.

"Are you on the pill?"

"Yes."

"Do I need a condom?"

Kelly shook her head. Her legs came up around his hips, wrapping around his waist and he could feel her heat against his cock, beckoning him to slide inside. He leaned over, covering one of her pert nipples with his mouth. As Chris sucked and tongued her, he took his cock in his other hand and rubbed it against her wet slit.

She squirmed beneath him, whimpers of pleasure escaping those full lips and he moved to her other breast, still teasing her with his tip against her clit.

"Fuck, Chris, now. Please, God, stop!"

Chris released her nipple and pushed his hips forward until his mouth hovered over hers, groaning as her body encased him in a sweet heat. He kissed her lips, watching her eyes roll up and close as he pulled out again and thrust forward. He held his body up on his forearms, pistoning hers with slow, steady strokes. Sweat broke out across his forehead and shoulders as he took his time, when all he wanted was to drive into her harder and harder.

Kelly's arms came around his shoulders and her breaths puffed against his chest. They grew shallower, faster, with a high-pitched sound on the end of every one, breathless little moans that drove him wild.

"Harder. Please. I'm almost…"

Chris pushed hard and her gasp turned into a scream when he did it again, getting off on her wild abandon. He closed his eyes, listening to her voice as she drew closer to paradise.

"Chris, yes, yes, please, fuck."

He opened his eyes and watched her fall apart. Her lips lush and parted, her eyes half closed, and her neck arched up.

She was so fucking beautiful, and she was coming for him. Because of him.

It was enough to send him over the edge. His hips jerked as he came, shouting her name as he let it all go.

It was the best sex of his life, and he wanted to stay in the moment. Connected to Kelly in a way he'd never been before.

It was Kelly who curled out from under him on her side, touching the lines of his face with the tips of her fingers.

"That was amazing."

He put his hand on her hip, and stroked her soft skin with his thumb.

"Yeah, it really was."

She leaned over, pressing her lips against his, and then pulled away with a grin. "I'm going to use the bathroom. If my legs will carry me that far."

He laughed as he watched her get up from the bed. Even in the darkly lit room, the light from the living room shone through, highlighting Kelly's curves like a spotlight. Her gorgeous ass swayed as she headed for the door.

"Turn on the light, would you?" he asked.

She did as he asked and stumbled a bit as she turned left out of the doorway and went down the hall. Once he heard the bathroom door shut, he lost his smile, staring up at the ceiling fan twirling.

What the hell had he started? He couldn't regret it, because he realized how bad he'd wanted it for so long. All his other girlfriends had seen it, his friends had seen it. Everyone knew he'd wanted Kelly but him. It was a story too old to even contemplate. A guy lusting for his best friend without realizing it?

Or he just hadn't wanted to know because the stakes were too high.

He rolled over to follow Kelly. Maybe he could convince her to take a shower, join her under the hot spray and run his hands over every inch of her beautiful body.

The light from the living room reflected off a picture collage to his left and he glanced over.

And stopped.

In between a picture of Kelly and her parents and Kelly standing in front of Something Borrowed was a picture from prom night. Ray and Chris stood on either side of Kelly. Chris's date had ditched him to get back together with her ex-boyfriend, and Kelly had refused to let him be alone. She'd waved him into the picture with Ray, who had been good-natured about the whole thing.

He could still remember Kelly's arm around his waist as the camera man had counted down.

"I'm so lucky. I have a date with two hot guys."

Ray and Chris had both laughed just as the camera flashed so their mouths were open, their teeth exposed as they looked down at Kelly, who was innocently smiling for the camera.

Chris stared at the three kids who had been inseparable. He'd never been able to replace Ray in his life. He had friends, buddies from college he'd talk to and catch up with, but Ray had been with him since kindergarten. They'd grown up together and he'd never have that history with anyone else.

He focused on Kelly, her hair piled on her head in a fountain of curls tumbling down around her face and shoulders. Ray had been her first love. She'd been planning to marry him. Chris knew he'd held her entire heart, so when it came down to it, would she really be able to move on? To give herself completely to someone else?

The bathroom door opened, and Chris ducked back into the bedroom. Kelly came around the corner just as he sat down on the edge of the bed. She stood in the doorway, beautifully naked and smiling shyly.

"Can I shut the light off?" she asked.

"Yeah, I'm just going to get cleaned up too."

"All right. Do you want to move this party upstairs?"

She was asking him to stay. She wasn't kicking him out or telling him this was a mistake.

"I'll meet you up there."

"Okay." She disappeared again, and Chris got up, shutting the light off when he left the room. When he finished in the bathroom, he climbed the stairs and found Kelly curled up under the covers with her back to him. He came around the other side, watching her breathe deeply.

Should he let her rest and sneak out the door? Or would she take that badly?

"Do you have to get home to Fungi?" she asked.

So, she was awake. "He's okay for a while."

"Then get in here and hold me."

Chris lifted the blanket with a laugh, and slid in until he was next to her. He wrapped his arm under her head and the other rested on her waist. She was tracing his chest with the tip of her finger over his skin and hair.

"Do you regret it?" she whispered.

He brought her hand up to his mouth and kissed it. "No. You?"

She shook her head. "I was afraid it would be awkward or terrible."

"Gee, thanks."

"But it was amazing, and I don't…I don't know what it means."

He kissed her forehead and then her nose, followed closely by her lips. He wasn't sure where they went from here either, but he didn't want to say that. There was so much to think about, so many ways this could go badly. Kelly was the most important person to him after his family, and he didn't want to think about what his life would look like without her in it.

"We don't have to decide today what we are to each other. Let's just be best friends."

"Who have seen each other naked?"

"Exactly."

She laughed, and snuggled closer. Within a few minutes, she melted into him and he knew she'd fallen asleep. He traced the curve of her hip with his hand, growing drowsy with her warm body pressed against his and the sweet smell of her hair drifting up to him.

*Chris walked down the hallway of El Dorado High School, wondering what in the hell he was doing there. The white halls were lined with blue lockers and although he remembered it as a loud, bustling environment, there was nobody there but him. It had been fourteen years since he'd graduated, and the place looked the same.*

*"Hey Chris," someone called.*

*He turned searching the empty corridor.*

*"Yo, in here."*

*Chris headed toward the voice, which was coming from a classroom to his left. He went through the doorway of to find the room empty.*

*It wasn't really empty though. At the front, behind the teacher's desk, sat Ray with his feet up on the flat wood. His hair was in a short 'fro, the way he'd styled it at the beginning of their senior year. His even white teeth flashed into a welcoming smile and his dark eyes twinkled.*

*"What's up, man? It's been a while. Although, I prefer this to your circus prom dream. That was just freaky."*

*Chris froze, shaking his head. "Are you real?."*

*Ray got up and came around to him. He was wearing the Raiders jacket Chris had bought him for his seventeenth birthday, even though Chris was a diehard 49ers fan. Ray gave him a one-armed hug, pounding him on the back and it felt so real, so good.*

*"Does this feel real?"*

*Chris tightened his hold on him. "Yeah."*

Ray tried to end the hug, but Chris held on. "Whoa, what's up with you?" Ray pulled away, eyeing him with confusion. "You act like I'm gonna die or something."

"You are, man. You're dead."

Ray grinned. "I know. Just fucking with you."

"Why are you here? Shouldn't you be in heaven or something?"

"Yeah, but you obviously needed me, or I wouldn't be here."

Chris glanced around the high school classroom. "This is a dream though, right? You're just a figment of my overactive brain."

"It's definitely a dream, but that doesn't mean I'm not actually here. Pretty sure I'm your guardian angel."

Chris laughed and shook his head. "Come on. We watched A Christmas Carol when we were kids and you said that was stupid."

"True, but when the man upstairs tells you that your best friend needs some guidance, you hop off that cloud. It's all about perspective, my friend."

Chris shifted his feet, uneasiness shrouding his joy. "So, you've been looking down on me?"

"Not just you."

The tone in Ray's voice was darker and Chris cleared his throat. "I'm sorry, man."

"Thanks for that. I mean, I understand. It's been a bit and you're both adults."

"But?" Chris asked.

"How is this going to work, with me between you guys? If I had never been in the picture, would you have come back when she asked you to? Would you have dated in high school, had a terrible break up and never seen each other again? Did you ever think that maybe I was in the picture, because I kept you two from doing something stupid, like hooking up?"

Anger ripped through Chris. "This wasn't just hooking up."

"No, it was almost twenty years of repressed hormones that exploded in a moment of weakness."

Chris assumed Ray was belittling Kelly and his connection because he was pissed and ran his hands over his head. "Look, I'm sorry. We didn't mean for this to happen."

Ray laughed. "Are you kidding me, man? I'm dead! Nothing I can do about it, and besides, I want Kelly to be happy. It's killed me watching her cut herself off...pun intended."

Chris groaned. "Your jokes were always terrible."

*"For real, man, I just want to make sure you know what you're doing. Because if you screw this up and break her heart, I will haunt your ass forever."*

Chris sat straight up in Kelly's bed, dripping with sweat. His heart pounded in his chest and his whole body shook.

"You okay?" Kelly asked, sleepily.

He turned to her and watched her lay there, her eyes closed and the moonlight from the window casting shadows across her pale skin.

"Yeah, I just got to get home and check on Fungi."

"Okay."

He climbed out of the bed and went downstairs to dress, still shaken from his dream, Ray's words replaying in his mind.

*Make sure you know what you're doing.*

He had no fucking clue.

# Chapter 20

Kelly woke up and stretched, her arms going out alongside her. When her skin pulled on her injured wrist, she winced, suddenly wide awake. She sat up, wiping at her sleep-filled eyes and sighed. Pepper, who was sleeping at the end of the bed, got up and arched his back, yawning. He padded toward her slowly, his purr loud and rumbling in his chest.

"Hey, my love. How are you?" she asked, her irritation with him from the night before forgotten as she stroked his soft, short fur.

Pepper rubbed against her, his tail shaking straight in the air.

"Yeah, me too." She felt amazing this morning, relaxed and happy. All thanks to Chris…

She frowned. Chris had gone to sleep with her. Where was he? Downstairs?

"Chris?" she called.

There was no answer, so she climbed out of bed and walked down the stairs. There were no cooking noises from the kitchen, the bathroom door was open, and he wasn't in the living room. She looked out the window and saw his car was gone.

He'd left without saying goodbye to her. Snuck out like a thief in the night.

That son of a bitch!

Kelly ran upstairs to get clothes on, furiously pulling on her jeans over a pair of bikini panties. She couldn't believe that Chris, of all people, would bail after sex.

She slipped a tank top on over her sports bra and went to get her keys from the counter downstairs. He was going to get a piece of her mind, and then some. Hitting and quitting your best friend was all kinds of wrong.

Kelly pushed the speed limit on her way out of Sweetheart and when she parked in front of Chris's house in Somerset, she was beyond reason. She marched up his porch and tried the knob, but it was locked.

So, she did what any woman would in her situation. She pounded on his door at six in the morning.

"Christian Thomas Ryan, you get your ass down here and open this door!"

*Bang! Bang! Bang!* She slammed her fist against the wood until it creaked under the weight. She was ready to pound some more, but she heard a rush of footsteps inside and Chris threw the door open, wearing nothing but a scowl and a towel.

"What in the fuck are you yelling about?"

"You left me!"

"What?"

She pushed him back into the house and closed the door behind her. "You made love to me and then left after. You literally hit it and quit it with me."

Kelly saw his mouth twitch and she pointed her finger at him. "If you laugh at me, you can kiss your balls good-bye."

Chris wiped all humor from his face and grabbed her other hand, which was still pressed against his chest. "I didn't ditch you. I woke you up an hour ago to tell you I was coming home to check on Fungi."

Kelly froze. "You did?"

"Yeah, and you said, 'okay.' I figured I'd get cleaned up and bring you back some breakfast. Then, change your bandage before you headed into work."

Kelly wracked her brain, but none of this was ringing any bells. "I don't remember that."

"Well, I did," he said, frowning down at her. "I can't believe you thought I would take off on you."

Her face burned with shame. "I'm sorry, I don't remember. I was just surprised when I woke up alone and there was no note. I thought...that maybe your regretted it and took off so you didn't have to deal with me."

"Geez, what the hell, Kelly?" He cupped her face in his hands and stroked her cheeks with his thumbs. "I swear, I said I was coming home. No matter what is going on with us, I would never hurt you. I thought you knew that."

Kelly did, at least, she thought she did. But this was her first time since Ray and she'd waited five years with him. They'd had a future planned. There was no plan with Chris. They'd slept together, and he'd said they would see where things went. It left her uneasy.

"I'm sorry. Of course, I believe you. This is just a first for me, and I don't know how to handle it."

"I told you, no matter what, we're still Chris and Kelly. We are still the same people we were before last night. No matter what happens, we need to remember that."

*But what are we together?*

She didn't ask though, mostly because she was scared that she didn't know what answer she wanted him to give. Everything was just getting more complicated, and she didn't like it.

"How's your wrist?"

"It's sore."

"I bet. Hang on, I'll grab you some Motrin." He kissed her forehead and pulled away. She watched him walk toward the kitchen, holding his towel up with one hand on his hip. She followed behind, some of the tension and worry disintegrating when she noticed the top of his ass was showing above the towel.

She almost tripped as Fungi ran under her feet after his master, meowing loudly. The little fiend glanced over his shoulder at her, giving her a snooty look as if to say, *"What are you doing here?"*

Chris grabbed a can of food from the cupboard and set it on the counter. "What's up, dude? You hungry again?"

"You wash your hands after you handle him, right?" she asked, thinking about his hands on her face and having a giant, red circle of ringworm show up there

"Of course, I do. His spots are already looking better, anyway. Been doing the cream four times a day, like the vet told me." He tossed her a pill bottle he'd pulled from the cupboard to her. "Get two and I'll pour you some water."

She sat down, watching Chris walk around the kitchen, taking care of her like he always did. But as much as she tried to pretend that they were the same old Chris and Kelly from yesterday, there was a major change she couldn't ignore.

Kelly now knew what Chris had going for him under that towel.

He set her glass down on the table in front of her. "There you go. I'm going to feed Fungi first, and then I'll head on up and put on some clothes."

*Or not.*

To her surprise, he squatted down in front of her just as she put the pills in her mouth. She took a sip...

"Or we could go back into my bedroom and have makeup sex."

She almost choked on the water in her mouth. Luckily, the pills went down, and she spluttered with water.

"What?"

"I was just thinking, we've had fights in the past as friends, but sex has never been on the table afterwards." He leaned close, his mouth right next to her ear. "Which means this should be really, really good."

His words sent shockwaves right to her core.

"What do you say, Kel?" His lips lightly trailed over the skin of her neck and she was lost.

# Chapter 21

Chris had every intention of telling her today that they shouldn't have had sex last night. That they should go back to being friends and not overly complicate things.

But that was before she'd come through the door, her eyes blazing with fury and hurt. Before her hands had touched his skin, and her gaze had traveled over him as though she couldn't look long enough.

All his good intentions had flown right out the window, and now here he was, carrying her into his bedroom, his towel in a wad on the kitchen floor.

"I should shower before we…" she whispered against his mouth.

"I don't care."

"I do. I feel gross."

"Not what a guy likes to hear when you're in his arms." He stopped at the edge of his bed, and let her slide down his body. "What about your arm?"

"The doctor said I could wash it, I just have to pat it dry."

"Okay."

He went into the bathroom and turned on the hot water, feeling her eyes on his ass as he waited for it to warm up.

Chris adjusted the temperature until it was this side of warm, and faced her, crooking his finger. "How's this?"

She stuck her good hand in, bringing her chest flush against his body. "It's perfect."

"Good." He stepped inside, and winked at her. "Care to join me?"

He watched Kelly pull off her tank top and bra in record time, and then kick off her flip flops. In her bare feet and chest, she shimmied out of her jeans and he couldn't help but stare at the way her tits jiggled with the motion.

Finally, naked, she unwrapped her arm and stepped in. He took her hand in his, turning it over so he could see the damage and he clucked his tongue. "Is the water too hot?"

"No, it's fine," she said seconds before she stood on her tiptoes and plastered her body to his. He caught the back of her head in his hands, kissing her deeply, turning her so her back was in the middle, the two streams raining down on them from either side.

Chris lifted her leg up and placed it on the step, giving him access between her legs. He poured some of his body wash in his hands and spread it over her collarbone, her shoulders. He avoided her arms, and moved onto her breasts, the bubbly suds leaving a trail as he swept his hands down her body. He rubbed over the short hair on her mound, and along the inside of her thighs.

The soap was gone by now and he slipped his finger into her slit, sliding one into her hot channel. Then two. She leaned her head back against the shower wall with a sigh and he kissed the side of her neck. Her shoulder. All the while he pushed three fingers in and out of her.

Chris used his thumb to press the button of flesh hidden in her folds and took her cry into his mouth as he kissed her. Warm water rained down on his back and head, sliding down his cheeks, and rivets trailed down over her breasts and belly. Chris quickened his motions, noting the tremble of her body as she drew close.

Without warning, he pulled his hand out and cradled her thighs in his hands, lifting her up and pressing her into the wall.

"I want you to come around my dick."

She laughed, throwing him for a moment until she breathlessly responded. "You're usually so polite. It's weird to hear you talk so dirty."

He pressed at her entrance. "Are you telling me to stop?"

She shook her head. "No. No, I love it. I love hearing you lose control."

Chris kissed her as he thrust inside, her muscles squeezing him tight.

"Mmmm," she murmured.

"Fuck, you feel better every time."

Her good arm went around his shoulder and he held her in place as he rocked against her, loving her hard nipples pressing into his chest. Her mouth under his, open and responsive, thrusting her little tongue against his as he slid in and out of her, feeling her muscles squeeze and quiver.

She let out a high-pitched moan in his mouth and tore her lips from his, screaming, "I'm there. I'm there. Fuck, yes!"

Chris sped up, long, hard thrusts as fast as he could move, catching up until he exploded inside her, shouting his joy and catching a stream of water in his mouth as he threw his head back.

"Jesus, Kelly, you're killing me."

Kelly's laugh was husky. "Hey, you're the one who wanted to shower with me. You could have just been patient."

"I've waited eighteen years to kiss you. I think I've been patient as hell."

He realized what he'd said aloud, and Kelly's eyes went wide.

"What?"

"Nothing, I'm just saying we've been friends and…"

"And you wanted to kiss me?" She stared at him with wide, earnest eyes. "Why didn't you ever say anything?"

He had a hard time meeting her gaze, especially since he was still hard inside her. He'd never talked about the times over the years where he'd been tempted to admit he wanted more from Kelly than friendship. First, it had been a betrayal to his best friend on every level. And then, there was the fact that taking that step with Kelly could potentially mean he'd lose her.

"Because every time I felt it, life got in the way."

Her hand stroked over his cheek and chin. "What about now? Why is it different?"

"I don't know," he said, honestly. "I think you telling me that you wanted to start dating pushed me to realize what I wanted. It was like a switch was flipped and I couldn't stand to think of losing you."

She frowned at him. "Losing me, how?"

"Eventually, you were going to meet someone, and they'd take up all your time. They'd resent our friendship and I'd slowly be reduced to just your lawyer, and then your husband wouldn't like even that, so he'd ask you to fire me, and then…hey, what's wrong?"

She was pushing him away frantically and he slipped reluctantly from her body, puzzled by the sudden change. Kelly reached over to turn the water off and left the shower, grabbing a towel from the linen closet.

"Hey, where are you going?" he asked, pulling his own towel from over the bar.

Kelly wrapped the towel around her body and turned around to face him, her features an angry mask. "You slept with me, so I wouldn't date anyone else?"

"What? No. That's not what happened. We got caught up in the moment and I"—her expression darkened and he realized he was only making things worse—"I don't mean that either."

"So, not only did you accidentally have sex with me, but you did it because you thought you would lose me?"

"No, Kelly, I *wanted* you. I still want you."

She jerked back when he tried to reach for her again. "Do you? I mean, what do you want from me? You've had years to tell me that. But you wait until now, until another man is interested in me?"

The mention of Hank Townsend pissed him off. "This has nothing to do with him. I was afraid to go here with you because I didn't want to risk what we have for something that won't last."

"Then why didn't you just tell me that the other night? Instead, you made me think...hope, that there was something more between us."

"There is, obviously! How can you deny it after the way we were together?"

Tears were pouring down Kelly's cheeks now and he wanted to hold her, to erase the pain he'd caused but she wouldn't let him near her. "I'm not talking about sex, Chris! I am talking about a future. You just admitted you weren't sure if there was one here and you were scared to take the risk."

"No one goes into a relationship thinking it's going to fail, but with us, we have more at stake. You are everything to me Kelly, and if I screw this up...I can't imagine my life without you."

A bitter laugh escaped her lips as she wiped at her eyes. "So, you're saying that you want me in your life, but you're just not sure I can be your everything? I can be your friend, or I can be your lover, but I can't be both?"

"I..." If he answered honestly, it was going to just make things worse, so he said nothing.

Kelly shook her head, and started gathering up her clothes. "You know, for a smart guy, you can be an idiot."

"Kelly, come on." He reached for her and she moved out of reach.

"Don't touch me. Not right now. I need space."

He backed up. "Okay."

Chris watched her leave, carrying her clothes against her chest. Every cell in his body was screaming to go after her, but he couldn't do that. If she needed time and space, he'd give it to her.

It was all he could do.

# Chapter 22

The next day, Kelly sat at Rylie's kitchen table, her arm held out for her to wrap. The adorable two-bedroom house Rylie rented was cozy, and warm, filled with knickknacks and decorations meant to make you feel comfortable. Kelly loved it here, especially because two of her favorite people were sitting with her.

Although, she wasn't a huge fan of having her bandage changed, since it hurt like a real bitch today.

Marley Stevenson sat next to her, sipping her coffee and watching silently. Her blond hair was pulled back in a braid, and her French-tipped nails clicked against the mug as Rylie placed the sterile pad with the burn cream on her wound. It was worse today, itching like crazy, and the skin under the peeling blisters was bright red.

"Ow! Dammit, be gentle," Kelly snapped.

Rylie took the gauze, holding the edge of the pad to keep it in place as she wound the medical supplies around her arm. "I am being gentle. You're just being cranky."

"You are kind of cranky," Marley agreed.

"I am not."

Marley set her mug down and clapped her hands. "Now, after that witty rejoinder, would you like to talk about what is really bothering you?"

Kelly glared at Marley. They'd known each other a long time, and while Kelly had been Marley's employer for seven years, they were also friends. Now, Marley did freelance editing for self-published authors and was doing well. She was also very involved in the Buzzard Gulch project, which was her baby.

Still, today was not the day to mess with Kelly.

"I think it has something to do with Christian," Rylie said.

"You, hush, or I'll find myself another baker."

Marley snorted. "Not one whose cakes taste as fantastic as Rylie's. At least not within a hundred miles."

Kelly pointed her finger at Marley. "You're annoying, you know that?"

"Seriously, I've never seen you like this," Rylie said, putting the green stretch wrap around the gauze. "What happened?"

Kelly did not want to talk about it, mostly because she felt like such a damn fool. She'd let her hormones get the best of her and jumped Chris. He'd given her every opportunity to run for the hills and she'd been like a puppy starved for affection. Coming off like a clingy, crazy woman. If she'd gone out with a guy for the first time, she wouldn't have slept with him and even after they did, she wouldn't have started in about their future. That would have been crazy.

She would have been cool. Given nothing away. At least, that's what she hoped she'd have done, because she hadn't been that way with Chris.

"Kelly?" Marley prodded.

Her friends sat there, staring at her like she was losing her damn mind. And maybe she was.

"Have you ever done something completely out of character?"

Both Rylie and Marley looked at each other and burst out laughing. Marley raised her hand.

"Got involved with the best man of a wedding I was working."

"And I fell I love with my co-worker at Something Borrowed," Rylie chimed in.

"So yeah, I think we've both done some things that were completely out of character, but only because they were the right thing for us." Marley cocked her head, studying Kelly. "What did *you* do?"

Kelly took a drink of her coffee and smiled sheepishly. "Chris. Twice."

Marley's jaw dropped while Rylie squealed, "I knew it! I knew you and Chris had the hots for each other."

"Yeah, but I don't really know if we do. He said he got caught up in the moment and that he was worried he was going to lose me to someone else."

"Excuse me?" Marley said.

"Yeah, and, he said he didn't know what the future would hold for us and is afraid of losing me if we don't work out."

"He gave you the 'your friendship means so much to me that I am afraid dating will ruin it' talk?" Rylie said.

Kelly and Marley turned to an outraged Rylie.

"That is the biggest load of horseshit!"

Kelly threw up one hand in solidarity. "That's what I said, but now I am wondering if I overreacted."

Marley shook her head. "Um, no. First, relationships are rough, and there is no room for cowardice. If you want someone, you must go for it, because they might not wait for you."

"So, do you want Chris?" Rylie asked.

"I don't know!" Kelly groaned. "I have no idea what I want. I mean, he's the person that knows me better than anyone. We have so much in common and we get along great together."

"How was the sex?" Marley asked.

Kelly blushed. "Pretty sure I had an out-of-body experience."

Both women laughed.

"Who started it?" Rylie leaned forward, her brown eyes sparkling.

Kelly pointed to her chest. "Me, I guess. I asked him to kiss me, which kind of set the whole thing in motion."

"Regardless of whether he can rock your world, you need to make him chase you," Marley said. "Right now, he thinks he's got you panting after him, and that isn't the case. He thought he could sex you into submission, so you wouldn't ditch his ass."

Rylie cracked up. "Sexed her into submission?"

Marley made an "o" with one hand and thrust her trigger finger through it in rapid succession, imitating sex. "Yes. He used his skills to make her forget that she had options. He needs to pay."

"Pay how?" Kelly asked.

"First, you need to figure out what *you* want from *him*."

Kelly thought about Chris. His smile. His eyes. The way he laughed. And the touch of his hands. The press of his lips.

"I want him to want to be with me."

"Okay. Time for plots and plans, then," Marley said, grabbing a pad of paper and pen from the counter.

"She needs some competition for him. Hank Townsend should be good at that," Rylie said.

"I don't feel comfortable including my client in this."

"Give him the option. He's an actor. He is perfect for the job," Marley said.

Rylie snapped her fingers. "Oh, and she is going to need to drive him crazy. She's got a great butt."

"Oh, yeah, and with the right bra, her boobs would just pop right up and say howdy."

Kelly waved her hands and made a time out symbol. "Whoa, whoa! I am right here, so stop talking about me like I'm not. I also don't think I need to tart myself up to get Chris to admit that he wants more with me."

"Fine." Marley set the pen down and folded her hands over the top of the pad. "What's your plan then?"

Kelly wracked her brain, but didn't have a single idea to contribute. "All right, I'll let you two work your magic."

# Chapter 23

On Thursday, Chris walked into Something Borrowed with a stack of new contracts. The office door opened up to reveal the large reception area with two desks and several comfortable chairs in various colors and styles. He'd planned on just leaving the pages with one of the receptionists, but he needed to see Kelly. He'd tried giving her space like she asked, but it was killing him. He hated when she was mad at him, and worse, the fact that she didn't think he cared, that he'd just used sex as an excuse to keep her close. It wasn't true. He'd made love to Kelly because he hadn't been able to stop himself, caught up in everything that he loved about her.

Chris walked down the hallways, plus several offices on either side to Kelly's, which was at the very end. He knocked on her closed door gently.

"Come in."

Chris turned the knob and stepped inside, only to halt in shock.

Kelly, her long dark hair loose, was hanging over the shoulder of Hank Townsend. Her low-cut shirt gave Chris a fabulous view of her breasts, and she hadn't looked up at him yet, but Hank saw him.

And the smug son of a bitch was grinning.

"Chris. Good to see you. We're going over the menu for the wedding. Kelly is trying to convince me to have a steak options on top of chicken, fish, vegetarian, and vegan, but I'm not sure. Thoughts?"

Kelly stood up, and he was struck by the smoky eyes and dark cranberry lipstick. He'd never seen her face like that. Her black top was tight and low-cut, the bottom flaring out over her hips. She had on a wide black belt, drawing attention to her slim waist. Hank was blocking the rest, but the change was so stark, he had to blink several times to make sure it was really her.

"You can leave the contracts on the desk," she said, coolly.

That knocked Chris out of his stupor and he set them where she'd pointed almost timidly.

"Sure." Very much aware of Hank's gaze following the two of them, Chris said, "Kelly, I was wondering if I could make an appointment to talk to you."

She shrugged nonchalantly. "You can check with my assistant, but I think I'm pretty busy until the Valdez wedding next week."

"And helping me plan my sister's wedding," Hank said.

Chris stood awkwardly, and the longer he was there, the more he wanted to punch Hank in his smug, stupid face.

"I'll check with your assistant. You two have a good day."

"You too, Chris," Kelly said.

Hank wiggled his fingers at him. "Toodle-oo."

He stepped into the hallway, closing the door behind him and didn't bother checking with Samantha. From Kelly's cold demeanor, she still hadn't forgiven him and wasn't ready to talk.

But damn, what was going on with her total makeover, stone-cold fox edition?

He left the building and headed back to his truck. This was his last appointment of the day, mostly because he'd thought that Kelly and he would have a lot to talk about.

Seems like he'd been wrong.

Chris drove home, and he couldn't shake the image of Kelly leaning over Hank, her hair basically falling into his lap. His hands tightened on the steering wheel. Was that what her new look was about? Was she taking it to the next level with Hank? It had only been five days since they'd been together!

He didn't like it. Didn't like that she could move onto someone new so fast.

Chris walked through the front door of his home, and as he passed by the couch, Fungi leaped onto the back of it and sprang at him like a tiny ninja assassin.

"Hey!" Chris caught him up in his hands, and held him a few inches from his face, giving the kitten a mock scowl. "You want a piece of me, small fry?"

Fungi's chest vibrated against the palm of his hand, reaching his paws out toward him in a stretch. It was as though Chris's very touch had rendered him lazy.

Chris tucked him in against his chest and walked into the kitchen, planning on making dinner.

His cell rang in his pocket and to his surprise it was Luke Jessup, Marley Stevenson's fiancée. Luke was a Sheriff's deputy and a nice guy who always invited him to poker night with a bunch of cops and Dustin Kent, but Chris wasn't in the mood to gamble tonight.

"Hey Luke. What's up?"

"Hey, man. Was gonna hit up Shotguns for burgers and beers. Wanna join me?"

Chris wasn't really in the mood for company, but beers and burgers sounded better than the leftover Subway sandwich in his fridge.

"Sure, when are you heading over?"

"I need about a half an hour to change out of my uniform and then I'm getting the hell out of dodge. Marley is hosting a book club tonight, and told me I need to vacate the premises."

Chris laughed. "Fun. What book are they reading?"

"Fuck if I know. All I do know is if I'm around while Marley has a group of women over, there is a good chance I'll be man-bashed."

"Pretty sure Marley loves you and wouldn't bash you."

"Yeah, but a lot of her friends are going through some nasty breakups and if they even catch a man's scent, they are like lions with an injured gazelle."

Okay, so maybe hanging with Luke would make him feel better. The guy was hilarious.

"All right, I'll change out of my uptight lawyer gear and meet you there."

"See you."

Chris ended the call and grabbed a can of cat food from the cupboard. Once he'd placed the nasty smelling meat on the plate, Fungi went nuts trying to get to it. He set both the plate and cat on the floor, then Chris went upstairs to change while he ate. He'd give Fungi his medicine when he got home.

Chris washed his hands before unbuttoning his shirt. As he slid the blue button off down his arms, something on his chest caught his eye in the mirror. He turned on the light and stepped closer, squinting to get a better look.

High on the right side of his chest was a red circle the size of a dime.

"Son of a fucking bitch!"

He had ringworm. His best friend hated him, was hooking up with a guy who was rich as hell, and now he had motherfucking ringworm.

He needed a drink. Stat.

Chris showered and after applying anti-fungal cream to his spot, dressed quickly. His black T-shirt rubbed against the ring on his chest and he had no idea if it was the fact that he knew about it now, but it itched like crazy.

He walked into Shotgun Wedding Bar and Grill a half an hour later and found Luke sitting at the bar, talking to Dustin Kent.

"Hey, guys," Chris said, sitting in the barstool next to Dustin.

"Hey," Dustin said.

Luke slapped Dustin on the back. "Hope you don't mind, but Rylie was going to book club, so I figured I'd invite this fool, so he didn't spend all night swimming in his millions."

Dustin laughed. "You seem to confuse me with Scrooge McDuck a lot."

"All I know is, if you don't stop taking my money at poker night, I'm going to shoot you," Luke joked.

"Or you could just stop inviting him," Chris said.

"Then I'll be described as petty. Can't have that."

"What can I get you?" the bartender asked. She was a pretty blonde Chris had never seen before and her sparkling blue eyes reminded him of the Pacific Ocean.

But that was as far as the observations went. "I'll take a beer, whatever they're having."

She winked at him. "Coming up."

She walked away, and Chris didn't realize that Dustin and Luke were both staring at him.

"What?"

"Did you see her smile at you, man? She wants you."

Chris shook his head. "Not really interested right now. Thinking of taking a break from women."

"Yeah right. Who is she?" Dustin asked.

"Who is who?"

Dustin took a pull of his beer before answering. "The chick you're hung up on."

"I'm not hung up on anyone."

Luke scoffed. "Right, which is why you aren't interested in hot blondes and why you're hanging out with us on a Thursday night."

The bartender came back with his beer and set it on the bar. "Here you go. That will be a buck."

"Why so cheap?" Chris asked.

She pointed to the chalkboard sign above the liquor shelf. "It's Thirsty Thursday. Dollar drafts until ten."

"Nice, thanks." He handed her a five. "No change."

She beamed at him. "Thanks."

She took off again and Chris laughed at the guys' skeptical expressions. "Jesus, you're as bad as Kelly. She thinks women hit on me everywhere I go."

Dustin chuckled. "Hey, we're both on the hook. We have to live vicariously through our single friends."

"Trust me, the single life isn't so great." Chris held his beer up, as though toasting. "It's complicated and messy. I'd much rather be with one girl, curled up on the couch watching Netflix."

Luke shook his head. "So, why are you swearing off women, then, if you want to get shackled like us?"

Chris wasn't used to discussing his problems with anyone but Kelly. Sometimes he would vent to his lawyer friends, but that was usually about work.

But it might be kind of nice to get other men's opinion about what was happening with Kelly, without naming names.

"Because I messed up bad with a woman I really liked and now I feel like a jackass."

"Gotcha." Dustin took a drink of his beer and continued, "As a former asshole—"

"What do you mean, former?" Luke teased.

Dustin pointed at Luke. "Fuck you." Luke cracked up and Dustin ignored him, focusing all his attention on Chris. "As I was saying, I messed up a lot with women and if she is the right one, she'll forgive you. Just tell her how you feel and see where the chips fall. If she tells you hell no, at least you know you tried."

"What if you aren't sure how *you* feel?"

"Then keep your mouth shut until you figure it out. No sense in getting a girl's hopes up."

Chris knew he was probably right about figuring out how he felt before bringing Kelly into it, but that was easier said than done. He'd tried to keep his distance and failed.

Which made one thing clear; he didn't *want* to stay away from Kelly.

# Chapter 24

Kelly sat in Marley's living room, sipping rosé and waiting impatiently for Luke to get home. Lying next to her on the couch was Marley's orange-and-white bunny, Butters, his eyes closed contently. She stroked her hand over his soft fur, a soothing gesture that actually seemed to calm her nerves.

Marley had convinced Luke to take Chris out and try to suss out what he was thinking. Luke wanted nothing to do with it, but Marley had convinced him it was in his best interest to play along. Kelly wasn't sure how and she really didn't need to know the details.

Rylie hadn't had to blackmail Dustin; he'd been delighted to go. Rylie joked that Dustin and Luke had a bit of a bromance going on.

Marley grabbed one of the lemon bars Rylie had brought. "So, what book were we supposed to read?"

"Sharla Lovelace's new one," Rylie said, holding the trade paperback up. "It was *so* good."

Marley spoke around a mouthful of food. "Right. I started it, and loved what I read, but I got two new manuscripts this week and was swamped with editing."

Rylie set the book down next to her with a sigh. "Why do we have a book club if I'm the only one who reads the books?"

Marley picked up her wine glass and held it up in a toast. "Because a book club is code for wine and girl time."

Kelly didn't join in on the fun, still thinking about Chris's expression today when he'd walked into her office. Maggie at the reception desk had called her office to let her know Chris had pulled in, so she'd jumped up and leaned over Hank, pretending to be showing him something closely.

Marley had told her it was trick guys did when they wanted to press up against a girl, but it usually had something to do with sports.

She hadn't expected Chris to look as though she'd kicked his kitten.

Kelly felt a little bad for messing with him, but she was hurting too. She'd washed her sheets on Sunday, wanting to destroy the evidence of their night together, but the pillow he'd slept on still smelled like his shampoo. She's spent the week cuddling with it, inhaling it whenever she got the urge to call him. Marley and Rylie had made it very clear she couldn't make first contact.

And Hank, well, Hank had been surprisingly cool. When he'd come by on Tuesday for their morning meeting, he'd apologized again for missing their dinner date, and asked when they could reschedule. She'd told him she enjoyed his company, but she couldn't. Something had happened, and she was no longer available. He'd been curious, so she'd explained the situation. When she'd told him about Marley's plan to make Chris jealous, he'd been more than happy to play along.

She was worried though that she might have pushed Chris too far. What if he wrote her off? Thought she was hooking up with Hank and had completely forgotten about what happened between the two of them?

The front door opened, and Luke Jessup stepped inside. Butters bounded to his feet, his big ears twitching with excitement before he raced down the wood ramp Marley had attached to the couch and skidded to a halt at his daddy's feet.

Luke picked the rabbit up and held him against his chest. "Are you causing trouble, bud?" He swept the room with his dark eyes, his large, imposing shoulders slumping when his gaze fell on Marley.

"I feel dirty," he said.

Marley jumped up and threw her arms around his neck from the right side so as not to squish the rabbit, kissing him passionately. When she pulled away, she smiled up at him as though he was the greatest man in the world.

"Baby, I am so glad you're home." She slapped him on his rear. "Now give us the dirt."

"Don't objectify me," he said, his lips twitching. "Do I need to tell you again that I am morally against this?"

Marley held up three fingers. "Three words. New Victoria's Secret."

He sighed. "He ignored the hot bartender who was trying to flirt with him, said he is swearing off women, and talked about a woman he really liked but blew it with." Luke looked right at Kelly. "Pretty sure he meant you."

Marley did a little victory dance. "Yes! You are the best."

Luke made a face as he set Butters down on the ground. "I am going to bed."

"I love you," Marley called.

He paused just outside their room with Butters close on his heels and gave her a heated stare. Kelly was sure that Marley's clothes were about to incinerate into a heap.

"Prove it," Luke said. "Say good-bye to your friends and come to bed."

He disappeared out of sight with his bunny sidekick and the click of a closing door was the only sound in the quiet living room. Rylie was looking up at the ceiling like she couldn't make eye contact and Marley grinned at Kelly, her cheeks bright red.

"So…"

"No worries, we're gone." Rylie stood up. "My place next week?"

"Sure. How about we do a thriller? I might even try to finish the book this time."

Rylie gave Marley a hug, rolling her eyes at Kelly. "Sure, you will."

Kelly guzzled the rest of her wine and stood up, giving Marley a hug. "Thanks for everything."

"My pleasure. Chicks before dicks."

"You're terrible," Kelly laughed.

"I'm hilarious."

They said goodnight and stepped outside together, while Marley closed the door behind them. The June sky was crystal clear, showing off the light purple hue that bled into black. The stars twinkled overheard as though winking at them. The moon was bright, very nearly full, and Kelly had no trouble seeing the ground as she made her way toward her car.

Rylie pulled out her phone. "I should text Dustin and see where he is."

"Yeah, and make sure Chris got home okay." She hated that she cared so much, especially since things were so screwed up.

Rylie leveled her with a pensive look in the moonlight. "You know, I think Marley's wrong about this plan. I mean, at first, I thought it was okay to let him know what he was missing, but if you really care about Chris, I don't think you should play games."

Kelly had been feeling the same way all day. If Chris didn't want anything more with her than friendship, she shouldn't push him into it.

"You're right. I'll talk to him tomorrow."

Rylie's phone beeped, and she laughed at whatever popped up on her screen. "We might actually need to get the guys now. Dustin said they are both pretty hammered and doing…" She squinted at her screen. "Karate? That can't be right. Why would they be doing karate at a bar?" Rylie looked up at Kelly with wide eyes. "You don't think they got into a bar fight, do you?"

"And their fight style of choice was karate? I doubt it. Autocorrect probably just made a mistake and he didn't notice." Since Kelly had only had the one small glass, she was fine to drive Chris home. "Let's go rescue our boys."

They climbed into Rylie's car and headed over to Shotguns. The short drive gave Kelly time to prepare herself for seeing Chris, inebriated and possibly mad at her, which would not be a great combination.

When they walked through the door a few minutes later, Kelly covered her mouth in surprise. On the stage with a microphone in his hand was Chris, singing a very bad rendition of "Friends in Low Places."

Next to him was Dustin, who could at least decently carry a tune.

"I think that text message was supposed to say *karaoke*," Kelly said, giggling.

Rylie squealed with laughter. "Oh my God. What are they doing?"

"I think they're singing," Kelly said.

"It's awful! Make it stop!"

Chris and Dustin were oblivious to their tone deafness, dancing around the stage like they were Luke Bryan and Jason Aldean rocking the house. When Dustin did a hip thrust, Rylie and Kelly wrapped their arms around each other. They were so weak with mirth they could hardly stand.

The song ended, and the room erupted with applause. Apparently, the more you drink, the more tone deaf you become.

Or their dance moves had scored them extra points.

"Hey, hey, that's my girl!" Dustin sang into the microphone. He put the mic on the stand and then came down the stairs to meet them at the edge of the crowd. Dustin wrapped Rylie up in a big hug and kissed her soundly on the mouth. "I missed you, sweetheart."

"I'm sure you did." She was smiling brightly, her face a mask of happiness only a woman in love could emanate. "You wanna explain what possessed you to get up on stage and shake your rear?"

Dustin waggled his eyebrows. "Chris dared me, and you know I never back down from a dare."

Rylie's cheeks turned crimson and Kelly didn't even want to know what that was about. She was happy for them, though. Rylie had been through the ringer, and although the rest of her friends had thought Dustin was just a douchebag, he'd actually turned out to be a pretty decent guy.

And he obviously loved Rylie, so that was a plus in his pro column.

Chris approached slowly, accepting back slaps and handshakes. The way the crowd was acting, you'd think he'd just won a major award, instead of taking a Garth Brooks classic and butchering it.

Chris stopped in front of her, giving her a sloppy smile, and she almost wished he would pull her into his arms like Dustin had done to Rylie.

"I'm so glad you're here," he said.

*Well, at least he's not pissed at me.*

"Yeah, I heard you could use a ride home."

"Why would you want to leave? We could do a duet together—"

"No!" Kelly and Marley said at the same time.

Chris turned to Dustin. "I don't think they liked our performance."

"And here I was going to suggest that we take this show on the road with merch," Dustin said.

"Okay, there will be no D&C merchandise, no music tour, and no more singing…ever." Rylie kissed Dustin and then patted his cheek. "Let's get you home and into bed."

"You take such good care of me."

Rylie rolled her eyes.

Kelly studied Chris as he weaved a little. "Are you going to make it to the car or do I have to carry you on my back?"

"Ha, that I'd like to see." Chris pulled his keys from his pocket and handed them to her. "I'd be okay if Dustin hadn't insisted on a shots-off. He got me drunk."

"Hey!" Dustin said. "I didn't know you were a lightweight."

"Come on, party animal," Kelly said. "We'll get you home and tucked into bed."

He slid his hand over her hair, surprising her.

"Why are you so good to me?" he asked.

So many reasons flashed through her head, but she didn't want to say any of them out loud in the middle of a crowded bar.

Instead, she played it safe, but spoke the truth. "You've always been there for me. Figured I'd return the favor."

"And I appreciate it." He leaned closer and spoke in a loud whisper. "I've seen Rylie drive and I don't trust her with my truck."

"Hey, I heard that," Rylie said.

"Sorry, but it's true." Chris reached out and took one of Kelly's long curls between his fingers. "I like your new look."

Kelly's heart beat picked up speed. "Thanks."

"Liked your old one too, though."

Rylie must have seen her annoyance, because she broke in. "Well, let's get them home before they decide to do some Journey."

"Journey sucks!" Dustin yelled.

"Shhh, are you trying to get us killed?" Rylie said.

They all walked out the door laughing, and down the steps. Kelly gave Rylie a hug goodnight when they stopped at her car. Then, Kelly laughed as she watched Dustin climb into the passenger seat, and pull Rylie in after him.

"Stop it, you perv!" Rylie cried, her voice thick with laughter.

Kelly didn't hear Dustin's response, but it would probably have shocked her. They reached Chris's truck and she unlocked the doors so he could climb in.

She got into the driver's seat, and after putting on her seat belt, started the truck up.

"Thanks for driving me home," he said.

"You're welcome." She backed out of the parking spot and pulled out into the road, her heart hammering. They were alone for the first time since everything went down, and even though he was drunk, it was still nerve wracking.

"So, you went to book club? You weren't out with Hank the Tank?"

Kelly laughed. "Um, yes I was at book club and no, no plans with Hank. And I don't think you should call him that. He might kick your ass."

Chris snorted. "What, you think he'd be mad? I don't care. I could take that pussy. He has to use a stuntman in his movies."

A giggle climbed up her throat. "And you do a lot of action movies, so you don't need one for your own action sequences?"

"No, smartass, I'm just saying that I could handle him in a fistfight."

She turned to stare at him briefly, her jaw hanging open. "Why would you hit Hank?"

"I almost hit him today."

"Because..."

"You were hanging all over him."

Well, Marley hadn't been wrong about the jealous part. "We were going over wedding plans! I swear, he's just a friend."

Chris snorted rudely. "That doesn't mean shit."

Kelly stiffened. "And what in the hell does that mean?"

"We were just friends when we slept together. Friends evolve all the time."

Kelly jerked the truck to the left, taking the turn onto his road sharper than she needed to, and he slammed into the passenger side door with a loud thump.

"Ow, what the hell?"

She turned on the four-wheel drive as the road turned bumpy. "Shut up. You're lucky I don't stop the truck here and make you walk the mile up the road. Let you get eaten by a mountain lion."

"What did I say?" he asked.

"Oh, besides the fact that I'm a slut that can't have guy friends because I sleep with all of them? I think that's enough."

Moonlight poured through the cab and she caught Chris's outraged expression out of the corner of her eye. "The fuck I did! I'm not that drunk!"

"You said that when I call a guy my friend, it means nothing because I slept with *you*. How else am I supposed to take that?"

Chris ran his hand over his face. "No, I...damn it, I didn't mean that. I can't say the right thing when I'm around you, especially when I'm not in my right mind."

"Then what did you mean?" she asked.

"I don't know. I have no idea what in the hell is going on! Everything has changed and is all messed up and why are you dressed like that?"

"Excuse me?" She slammed on the brakes before she plowed through his porch, and he jerked forward against his seat belt, his nose nearly hitting the dash.

"Jesus, maybe I should have let Rylie drive!"

"What did you mean *why am I dressed like this*?"

He seemed oblivious to the fact that he was in dangerous territory, because he answered. "I mean the tight clothes and the makeup. It's not you."

*Oh my God, I am going to beat his ass.* "How I look is none of your business!"

"Yeah, but you don't need it. You don't need all that crap on your face and your boobs hanging out to be beautiful."

Although that was almost sweet, it still didn't make up for everything else he'd said. "Get out."

"Huh? It's my truck."

"And I *might* bring it back to you tomorrow, but right now, I am tempted to run you over with it!"

Chris smirked at her. "Then I should probably stay here."

"No," she growled. "I want to go home before I hurt you."

He cocked his head to the side, so adorably confused...dammit, she hated that she thought he was still adorable.

"Why are you so mad?" he asked.

How did he not understand? She laid her forehead on the steering wheel, fighting back tears. "Because you criticize the way I'm dressed and how much make-up I'm wearing. And then you tell me you don't believe me when I tell you Hank is just a friend and everything you said to me last weekend...I just don't like you right now."

Kelly heard his seat belt snap open and felt his warm hand on her back through her shirt. She tried to shrink away from his touch, but there was nowhere to go. Soon, her shoulders were shaking with emotion.

"Kel, I'm sorry. You look great no matter what, and I didn't mean anything by it." He scooted as far over as he could get with the middle console and pulled on her, until she gave in and let him wrap his arms around her. "I just didn't like seeing you all over that guy."

"There is nothing going on with Hank and me. I'm not the type of girl who jumps from one guy to the next. You should know that about me."

"I do. I just..."

He didn't say anything else and she looked up at him, her vision blurred because of the tears threatening to spill over.

"Aw, don't cry, sweetheart. You know I hate it when you cry."

She tucked her hair back behind her ear and a single tear fell over her lashes and down her cheek.

"Why didn't you like seeing me all over Hank?"

He smoothed his thumb over her cheek and she felt the wet spread of her tears across her skin.

"Because."

She laughed softly. "That's not a reason. That's a school yard excuse."

He smiled at her. "Now who's being insulting?"

Kelly covered his hand and held it to her cheek. "Please, no jokes. Just be honest with me."

Chris took a deep, shuddering breath and met her gaze. "I was jealous. I don't want him touching you, ogling you...pretty much any action that involves you."

"Why?" she asked.

"Because I don't want to see you hurt. I hate that I've been the cause of any of your pain."

Chris's words softened her anger and she found herself stroking over his cheek with her fingers, the sharp scratch of stubble tickling the pads. "What do you want then?"

Without warning he lunged at her, taking her mouth with his. The burst of sensation made her cry out, and cling to him, opening her lips under the press of his tongue. Lightning-hot flashes of desire raced through her veins and she melted against him.

When he finally pulled back, with his lips a hairsbreadth away, he answered.

"You," he growled. "I want you."

## Chapter 25

Chris cupped the back of Kelly's head, kissing her with every repressed emotion he'd been bottling up for days. When she pushed against his chest for a moment, he let her pull back enough to speak.

"We shouldn't do this right now. You're drunk."

He shook his head, brushing his lips against her cheek while her mouth was turned away. "I'm not that drunk. I have ninety percent of my faculties. I know you're Kelly, I know you taste like some kind of sweet wine, and I know I never get tired of kissing you."

He let out an *oof* as Kelly climbed across the middle console and straddled his lap, her lips covering his.

Chris slid his hands up her back, gripping her through the fabric of her shirt. Her pencil skirt rode up to her waist. Her hands framed his face as she kissed him, and he opened his mouth under hers. She ground down on him in response, and his erection pressed painfully against the front of his jeans.

This is what he'd been dreaming of for days. Kelly, wild in his arms, desperate to be with him. He'd done everything to try not to think about her, naked and quivering against him, crying out with passion. He'd thought he'd be strong enough to not want her, to make things right so they could go back to being friends.

By the way his cock was straining to be inside her, he knew he'd failed big time.

He slid one of his hands between them and found her wearing a thin satin thong, barely enough fabric to cover her.

"Do you love this underwear?" he asked.

She shook her head.

He used both hands and ripped it out of his way. Then, he went to work on his belt and jeans. His motions were so frantic, his hands shaking, and then hers were tangled in the mix. Together, they managed to push everything down to his knees until his cock was free. He rocked his hips against her wet folds and a hiss escaped between his lips. Kelly rubbed against him, working her body until the tip of him slipped inside. She whimpered above him, and he groaned at the sensation as her body sucked in the head of his cock. Then she was rocking her way down his length until he was all the way inside her, and he shuddered in ecstasy.

For some reason, the shake of Kelly's hips on top of him seemed to ring a confession from him.

"I didn't mean it when I said that I thought what we did was a mistake."

"You didn't?" God, her voice was so hot. Breathless and slightly smoky, it made his dick flex.

"No. It was the best night of my life; how could it be a mistake?" He gripped her hips in his hands and thrust up hard.

Her hips jerked, and her breath hitched. "Why did you say it, then?"

Chris repeated the motions slowly, listening to her uneven little gasps. "So many things. Scared of losing you. Of betraying Ray."

She stilled on top of him. "Ray? You think we're betraying Ray?"

The shock on her face told him she'd never considered it before, but she was doing so now. Shit.

He pressed his forehead to hers. "I don't know. You were his girl for so long. It felt as though I was horning in on his territory."

Kelly's expression snapped into a scowl. "Wait, I'm a territory now? Like a land to be conquered and claimed?"

He held her hips fast when she started to climb off him. "I didn't mean that. Ray loved you and you loved Ray. I'm worried that you need someone with a clean slate, so there is no comparison or constant reminder of what you lost. Anything we have will always be tied to him, and I just…I don't want you to want me because it brings you closer to him."

Kelly stared at him with something he could only describe as disbelief. "Are you serious?"

"I wouldn't joke about this."

"I never thought of our friendship as tied to Ray. We might have grown close because of him, but we've stayed tight because of *us*. And you're right, I did love Ray. I will always love Ray, because he was my first everything. But I don't want to be tied to his loss for the rest of my life. I want to be happy." She stroked the side of his face tenderly. "And when you aren't being an idiot, you make me very happy. I don't think of anyone but you when we're together."

Chris's chest expanded as a rush of air blew out of him. He hadn't even realized he'd been holding it, waiting for what she would say.

Using his hands still on her hips, he made her sway, his cock still buried inside her. "Do you want me to make you happy now?"

She slid her arms over his shoulders and smiled. "Yes, please."

Chris held onto her to get her going, slowly bringing her down as he pushed up. Before long though, she'd taken over, finding her own rhythm. He leaned back against the seat, lifting his hips as she pushed forward, watching her under hooded eyes as she found what she liked, what felt good to her. He loved the look on her face when she hit the right spot, her mouth forming a little "oh" as she repeated the motion. Her head falling back and her eyes closing.

It was fucking beautiful.

Before long, she was crying out in pleasure, her muscles spasming on his cock and her body quivering in his arms. He kept thrusting up into her, finding his own release as she came down from her orgasm, her mouth pressed softly against the side of his neck. He groaned in satisfaction as he came.

"Kelly, fuck."

His body jerked once, twice, and when he was spent, he held her loosely against him, trying to catch his breath.

She placed little kisses up his neck and jaw, rubbing her cheek against his. "That was pretty good."

He opened one eye, and caught her grin. "Really? We've gone from amazing together to pretty good?"

"Only because the close quarters are giving me a leg cramp."

Chris realized that the seat belt clip was digging into his left butt cheek and winced. "I feel your pain."

He opened the door and helped her off his lap and out the door. Once all his parts were back inside his pants, he got out of the truck. They stood in front of his place, under the moonlight and pine trees, and fighting back the doubts and fears, he took her hand.

"Do you want to come inside?" he asked.

"I do, but I don't want to move too fast." When he laughed, she grinned sheepishly. "I mean, any faster than we already have. I think that's what happened the first time. We hadn't even kissed before and we jumped into bed."

"Right, and riding me in the front seat of my truck is going slow."

She shoved his shoulder with her free hand. "Shut up."

He pulled her closer since her hand was still in his. "I really missed you, Kel."

"I missed you too."

Chris tugged her toward the porch. "Then I think you should come in."

She held back. "Wait. First, before anything else happens, I wanted to apologize about pressing you so hard about what we were last weekend. It all came out of nowhere and you weren't the only one freaked. I was just surprised because I've never...felt that before."

"Felt what?"

"That kind of passion. That out of control 'I need to be near this guy' sensation."

Chris kissed her, his hands coming up to tangle in her hair. "I haven't either. It wasn't just you. I really want to give this a try, Kelly. Not because I am trying to keep you from experiencing life, but because I want to share it with you."

"Wow. That was pretty romantic."

"Is that a yes to spending the night with me?"

She smiled brightly. "Yes."

They climbed the porch steps hand in hand and when they got inside, Chris pointed to the spare bathroom.

"If you want to get cleaned up, I'll use the master bath."

"Sure. Can I borrow a T-shirt to sleep in?"

Chris pressed his mouth against her ear. "You're not going to need it."

Kelly blushed. "Naughty."

"Uh huh, so hurry up."

Kelly disappeared into the bathroom. Chris went into his bedroom and stripped off his clothes. Fungi watched him from his perch on top of the cat tree Chris had bought him, his eyes heavy lidded with sleep.

Chris put the anti-fungal medicine on his little circle and then covered it with a bandage before Kelly walked in. After he washed his hands and brushed his teeth, he got into bed.

Kelly came in a few minutes later, wearing nothing at all and his breath caught as her hips swayed the entire way across the room. She crawled across the bed and stopped, frowning as she pointed to his chest.

"What is that?"

He glanced down at his bandage. "It's nothing."

"Then why do you have a gauze pad on it?" she asked.

Chris groaned. "Fine. I have ringworm."

Her mouth dropped. "You weren't going to tell me?"

"It's not like I have herpes. I have it covered, and you said it was no big deal."

"Nope. That stuff is so contagious. There is no way I am sleeping in this bed with you."

She started to scramble back, and he caught her, pulling her under him while he hovered over her. "Hey, you have already been in my bed once and you've handled Fungi, so if you were going to get it, it would have happened already."

She stuck her tongue out at him, but stopped struggling. "You are so lucky I like you."

Once he was sure she wasn't going to bolt, Chris laid back on the bed, waiting for her to snuggle against him. On his unaffected side.

The alcohol hit Chris harder as they lay there, breathing softly, his hand stroking her skin.

"I love you," she whispered.

"I know," he mumbled automatically, just before he drifted off to sleep.

*Chris sat on an old swing, like the one at the park Ray and he had played on as kids. He kicked his legs in the air as he went higher and higher.*

*"You better not jump or your mom's gonna be mad."*

*Ray's voice startled him, and he dragged his feet to stop, staring at his friend next to him. Ray was wearing his big, blue parka and Sacramento Kings beanie he'd worn throughout fourth grade, but looked like he did at twenty-one. His hair was shaved close to his scalp and underneath he wore his standard army fatigues.*

*"You scared me."*

*"Sorry, just figured we wouldn't have much time to talk. It's gonna rain soon."*

*Chris squeezed Ray's shoulder. "I know you were worried about me hurting Kelly, but we're good."*

*"Really?" Ray's voice was thick with skepticism.*

*"Yeah. I told her some of my concerns and she voiced her frustrations. It's great."*

*Ray stood up on the swing, arching his body to go higher. "So, when she told you that she loved you, something that she's never said to another man since me, how did you respond?"*

*Chris tried to remember what Ray was talking about, and suddenly, the memory came rushing back.*

*"I said 'I know', but she didn't mean it like that. She was just doing our bit."*

*Ray watched him around the chain of the swing, his face shifting from left to right. "How did you know she didn't mean it? Did you ask her?"*

"Well, no, but she would have said something if she did, right?"
Ray shook his head. "You, my friend, have a lot to learn about women."
Suddenly, Chris panicked. Did Kelly really love him? Was he in the same place as her emotionally? And if he wasn't, how did he come back from that?
"What do I do?"
Ray jumped from the swing and landed in a crouch, breathing hard. When he stood up and face him again, his expression was blank. "That's up to you. Do you love her?"
"Of course, I love her. This is Kelly we're talking about."
"No, I mean, do you love her in the 'til death do you part' kind of way?" Ray asked, punctuating each word with his hand. "Because that is what she is looking for and if you can't give her that, you should let her go."
"What if I can't?"
Ray watched him sadly, and Chris gripped the chains on the swings as large, white wings spread out from the back of Ray's jacket.
"Then you were never the guy I thought you were."
Ray turned his face up to the sky and with bent knees, shot upward. The ground shook beneath Chris and Ray disappeared into the clouds.
Chris woke with a start, and reached out to pull Kelly closer, but his arms touched nothing.
He got up, searching the house and calling her name.
She was gone.

# Chapter 26

On Friday morning, Kelly tapped her pencil onto her desk, the steady beat strangely comforting. She hadn't been able to keep any part of her body still, especially her brain, after last night.

She still couldn't believe that she'd told Chris she loved him. Like, *really* loved him, and he hadn't realized it. He'd just mumbled, "I know," and a few moments later had been passed out snoring. She could have ignored it, and pretended it was no big deal, but in the end, she'd called Rylie and asked her to come get her. The last thing she'd wanted was to take off with Chris's truck after ditching him.

Her phone beeped, and she pressed the intercom button. "Yes?"

"Ms. Barrow, your mother is on line one."

Kelly was a little surprised her mother was calling on her work phone instead of her cell, but pressed line one with a smile.

"Hi Mom, how's the desert treating you?"

"Hot as the blazes, but that's why God made air conditioning."

Kelly knew her parents loved Arizona, no matter how they complained about the heat. They'd followed Kelly's uncle and his wife there when they'd retired and had become quite the social butterflies. Kelly had been upset when they'd told her they were moving, but as they pointed out, they saw her more now than when they lived five minutes away from her.

"Pretty sure air conditioning is manmade."

"God can take credit for all of man's accomplishments," her mother admonished.

"Yes, you're right. So, what's going on, Mom? You called my work phone in the middle of the day, so something has to be up."

"Well, I'm so glad you asked." Why did she sound so cheerful? "I wanted to tell you that your father and I have decided to celebrate our fortieth wedding anniversary renewing our vows. In *Hawaii*."

Kelly's eyebrows shot up. "But...your anniversary is in three weeks."

"Yep."

Kelly groaned, cupping her forehead in her hands. "Mom, you can't plan something like that in so short a time."

"Actually, we've been planning this for a while, this is just the first time I'm telling you about it."

*Oh, God, why is she doing this to me?* "But why? Why wouldn't you tell me, so I could be there? I mean, I have a business and I have to prepare for these things."

"Well..."

"And I could have helped you! How long are you planning on being gone?"

"We're going to do five days with friends and family and then ten days just the two of us. Like a second honeymoon."

Kelly could feel a headache starting behind her forehead. "All right, well, I guess I'll have to see if I can get a flight and hotel room in..." Kelly looked at the calendar and groaned. "The first week of July that won't bankrupt me."

"Oh, don't worry about it, honey! That's taken care of, as is your schedule. I called Veronica months ago and she promised me she'd keep your schedule clear."

Kelly stared at the phone, wondering if she could telepathically choke her mother. "You...conspired...with my assistant?"

"Yes, and I have to say, she is a lovely girl. I think you should promote her to a consultant. Smart as a whip, that one."

Kelly was going to have to have a companywide meeting about her employees being in cahoots with her mother. And how that was a *bad* thing.

"Oh, and Marcy and Keith are coming."

"Chris's parents?"

"Yes! Marcy is one of my dearest friends, and of course, Christian was invited. Such a lovely young man."

"He's thirty-two, Mother."

"And when you are sixty-four, that is young."

Kelly attempted to sound casual as she asked, "Did he say he'd come?"

"I believe so, at least, that's what Marcy told me. I really wish you'd wake up and just marry him already. A man like that, driven, successful, *handsome*...well, he won't wait forever."

Kelly didn't want to tell her mother what had transpired between her and Chris or she might trigger overprotective mama mode. There were some serious drawbacks to being the only child of a woman who would do anything within her power to make her child happy. Her mother was a fixer, and although it was wonderful in some instances, personal relationships were not the place for it.

"Chris and I are just fine where we are, but Mom, you really need to realize that I'm an adult. I don't need you to buy my plane ticket or hotel room."

"I know, baby, but I wanted to be sure that you wouldn't get sucked into some kind of work emergency."

Did her parents actually think she would put work before them? "Never. You guys are celebrating a huge milestone and I wouldn't miss it for anything. But for your fiftieth, please don't spring a skydiving trip over the jungle on me, okay?"

"You got it, baby! I'll email you all your travel itinerary, and don't worry. I know you're a genius when it comes to weddings, but the hotel has assured me that both the photographer and planner come highly recommended."

"Is this going to be a full-on ceremony or..."

"Oh, I need to run, honey, but yes, you're going to be my maid of honor. Veronica promised to pick up your dress next week so if there are any last-minute alterations, we can get those done."

"Well, I love you."

"I love you too, honey! Talk soon."

Kelly hung up the phone and pressed the intercom. "Send Veronica in to see me when she gets back."

"Yes, Ms. Barrow."

Kelly clicked off and groaned, resting her head on her desk. When had her life become an awful romantic comedy? Sure, her love life was in shambles, but at least her parents got to renew their vows and have another romantic trip, while she had yet to have one.

God, she shouldn't be like that. Her parents still loved each other after all this time. They deserved to celebrate forty years.

Someone knocked at her door, destroying her mild pity party.

"What?"

Rylie poked her head in. "Bad time?"

"Yes, but if you've brought something sinful with you, I will forget all about it."

Rylie pushed the door open and held up a plastic container. "Your wish is my command."

Rylie set it on her desk and popped the lid off, revealing an assortment of mini cupcakes. They all had brightly colored frosting swirled on top, and Kelly's mouth watered.

"What are these for?"

"I thought I'd do this for tastings from now on. This way, we waste less cake and it isn't so messy for some of the more...high-maintenance brides."

"I like it. Speaking of high maintenance, my mother called me a few minutes ago."

"Yeah? What's happening?"

Kelly pulled the wrapping off her cupcake, a chocolate concoction with red frosting. "My parents are celebrating their fortieth anniversary in Hawaii by renewing their vows."

"Oh, how romantic!"

Kelly made a face. "Yeah, except they didn't tell me. She just went behind my back and arranged everything with Veronica. Told her to keep my schedule open. As though I didn't handle wedding arrangements professionally and couldn't help her."

"Maybe she wanted to do it her way and was afraid you'd take over?"

"I don't take over! Do I?"

Rylie watched her thoughtfully, as if gauging her response. "Well, sometimes you get very...assertive with your opinion. But in a good way."

"How can that be taken in a good way?"

"All right, forget I said that. Perhaps she went behind your back because she knows you're very busy and that can sometimes make you distracted. Maybe she just wanted to make your life easier?"

"Maybe. She's organized for Chris's parents to come...and Chris."

"And is this good?"

Kelly sighed loudly. "It would be...except I told Chris I loved him last night."

"Oh wow. I was wondering why you called me so late for a ride. Why didn't you tell me? What did he say?"

"He said, *"I know."*"

Rylie's dark eyes narrowed. "Um, no he didn't."

"Yeah, but it's kind of our thing. It's the Princess Leia and Han Solo bit. So, I don't think he thought I was serious, but still it was painful to just lay there next to him."

"I can imagine. I'm sorry, Kelly."

Kelly took a bite of her cupcake, sighing over the sweet frosting and light, fluffy cake. "It's okay. I was just laughing because here I am, months away from being thirty-two, and I feel like I'm only twenty in dating years. I'm years behind everyone else. Plus, Chris and I keep having misunderstandings and I am just so tired of trying to figure out what the heck is happening between us."

Rylie shrugged. "I always thought Chris was really smart, but now, I'm convinced he might be a dumbass."

Kelly didn't really think Chris was purposefully being obtuse. She was pretty sure after their talk last night there was deeper stuff going on.

"I think it could just be that we aren't in the same head space. Cassidy broke up with him less than a month ago and I know he said it wasn't working, but maybe he's still hung up on her. That would make sense. Meanwhile, my feelings for him have been growing stronger every year, with no one else except him in my life. No men, I mean."

"I get it. I always had a feeling there was more between you and Chris, but I thought you two were just keeping it on the down low," Rylie said. "Still, I think Chris is right there with you. I've seen the way he watches you. Maybe he's just scared?"

"Last night, he told me he was afraid I couldn't love anyone else as much as I loved Ray."

"Is that true?" Rylie asked.

"No." How could she explain it without trivializing the seven and a half years she'd been with her first love? "I loved Ray with my whole heart, and would have married him, built a life with him. He took a part of me with him when he died, and he was hard to get over. But what I feel for Chris is…more mature? It's had time to grow and now, I want him to just realize that I made room for him a long time ago without realizing it. That there is no competition."

Rylie drummed floral print-painted fingernails on Kelly's desk, her eyebrow quirked. "So maybe you should have stayed last night and explained that this morning, instead of running off?"

"Okay, I don't need you to be a smartass."

"Sorry, but every time Dustin and I have had issues, it's because one of us wasn't being honest and open about how we were feeling. I truly believe that everyone's lives would be better if we just talked to each other instead of being so scared."

The scene from *A Few Good Men* flashed through Kelly's mind as Jack Nicholson screamed, *"You can't handle the truth!"*

Still, Rylie was right. Everything that had gone wrong with Chris and her had happened because they couldn't put what they were feeling into words.

"I'm trying to follow your advice, but it is hard."

"Everything worth having is hard to get. If it were easy, the results wouldn't be as rewarding."

Kelly laughed. "Okay, did everyone in my life take a class in how to make inspirational quotes?"

"Nope. I just spend way too much time reading Facebook memes."

# Chapter 27

On Friday afternoon, Chris stood over Ray's grave, reading his headstone for the hundredth time.
*Raymond Charleston Jackson*
*Beloved Son. Brave Soldier. Honorable Friend.*
Chris's eyes pricked with tears as he squatted down and put his hand on the top of the headstone, just like he used to do to Ray's shoulder. The sun beat down on him, alerting him that the ungodly hot weather of summer was fast approaching. Yet the green lawn of the graveyard would never turn yellow like the rest of the plant life in Sweetheart. In fact, the ground squished under his feet, and water droplets clung to the blades of grass around him.

He had no idea why he'd come here today. It was crazy and sentimental. Except that he'd just needed to talk to his best friend and this was as close as he could get to Ray.

"Hey, man. I know it's been a while since I've been here. Although, I'm kind of convinced that it is really you visiting me in my dreams. If I'm right, give me a sign." He stood back up, looking around for a cool breeze or some imaginary being to punch him in the shoulder, but nothing happened. Still, he kept talking. "Anyway, if you really have been looking down on me, and those dreams weren't all in my head, then you know that Kelly and I have feelings for each other. And I want to apologize. This is something that happened. Neither of us planned it, but I'm struggling with everything. I don't know why I'm so nervous about being with her, but I am. All I keep thinking about is that if we don't work out, things won't be the same. Then I realize it's already too late; we've already reached the point of no return."

Chris wiped at his eyes when his vision blurred, and he realized he was crying, that tears were falling down over his cheeks. "Damn Ray, I really miss you. There was never anyone like you. I'm making friends though, trying not to be such an antisocial loser. But...none of them have our history. No matter how cool they are, they can never be you."

The snap of a twig behind him startled him and he turned to find Ray's mother, Grace, watching him with a small smile. Her long black braids were pulled up away from her face, strands of gray highlighted in them now. She wore a loose, floral dress that ended just above her ankles, and gladiator sandals encased her feet. She was holding a flower in a pot, her dark eyes sad.

"I'm sorry, Chris. I didn't want to intrude."

He tried to erase the evidence of his emotional meltdown with his sleeve. "Mrs. Jackson, not at all. I was just checking in with him. Making sure he knew he was missed."

She stepped up beside to him and set the plant down next to Ray's headstone. Then, she straightened up and pulled Chris in for a tight hug, her head barely coming to his shoulder.

"My boy was lucky to have such a good friend."

Chris hugged her back. He'd spent so many dinners and birthdays with her family, and she had always treated him like a second son. "I was lucky too, ma'am."

When she pulled away, her cheeks were wet. "How's Kelly? I haven't seen her since Mother's Day."

Chris was surprised. He'd had no idea Kelly still visited Mrs. Jackson, and it made him feel all the worse for not making an effort to check on her and her husband more. "She's good. Busy with Something Borrowed, as usual."

"Oh, yes. Max and I are so proud of her for everything she'd accomplished. Ray would be proud of her too." Mrs. Jackson seemed to hesitate, then asked, "Is she seeing anyone?"

"Um...yeah, she is."

Although she smiled, Grace's eyes held a deep sadness that caused an ache in Chris's chest. "I am so glad. I mean, I was always grateful for the devotion she showed my son, even after he was gone, but Ray adored her. He'd want her to be happy." Grace met his gaze searchingly. "Is she?"

"Happy?" he asked.

"Yes."

Chris nodded. "She's getting there, I think."

"Good." She patted his arm, and shot him a teasing grin. "What about you? Still seeing that doctor?"

"No, I...well she broke up with me."

Grace clucked her tongue sympathetically. "Oh, I am sorry. You'll know when you meet the right girl. She will bring out all the good things in you and you'll do the same for her. Just be sure when you find her that you never let her go."

Chris's mind strayed to Kelly and his dream of Ray.

"Mrs. Jackson, I'm...I'm the one seeing Kelly."

A shadow passed over her face briefly, but it was swiftly gone, replaced by a tender smile. She squeezed his arm, a supportive gesture he was sure was meant to assure him she was fine with it. "I was wondering when that was going to happen."

"You knew that Kelly and I were going to get together?" He was a little surprised by that, considering it had taken them so long to realize it themselves.

"Not before Ray died, but after...it was obvious, at least to me. You took care of Kelly when we lost Ray. We all had our own grief, and supported each other, but you absorbed hers into your own. You were her strength when she needed it and I knew then that eventually, Kelly would realize what an amazing thing it is to find love twice in a lifetime. Like I did."

Chris stared at her. "I didn't know you were with anyone but Mr. J." Her husband had been a P.E. coach at the middle school and everyone had called him that.

"It was before I married. I was a sophomore in high school and he was a senior. I was mad for that boy, let me tell you. But he joined the army. He was supposed to get leave to come to my high school graduation, but instead, his best friend came by to let me know that he had been killed in a car accident on his way home to me."

Chris was enthralled and wondered if Ray had ever heard this story before. "Oh, man. I am so sorry. Wasn't Mr. J in the army too?"

She smiled softly. "Yes. He was my sweetheart's best friend. Neither of us planned it. He sent me letters, at first telling me stories about him and my David. Soon, it became more. Our hopes and dreams. Then, one night, he showed up on my doorstep with his duffel bag and his discharge papers. He told me that he wanted to tell me in person that he was in love with me. A year later, we were married, and then nine months after we had Ray."

"Wow. Did Ray know?" he asked.

"No, I never told him that story. He knows David was his dad's best friend, but he didn't know that my love for David was how we met. Life sometimes has tragic ways of bringing two people together and making something beautiful."

Chris was blown away by her understanding, and blurted out, "I...I haven't been able to tell her...that I love her, I mean."

"Why ever not?"

"I don't know. I keep dreaming of Ray for some reason and he keeps telling me to man up or let her go."

She laughed, wiping at her wet eyes. "That sounds like something he'd say."

"Yeah. I don't know, I guess I thought maybe visiting him would give me clarity? I know that sounds stupid."

"Well, I don't know. I come here to talk to him as well, usually on Sundays. Today I was headed to the market and it was almost as though he was asking me to come." She stepped closer to the headstone, running her hand over the top as though she was stroking her son's cheek. "I always feel he's with me, but there is something about here...I sense him."

Chris thought about how moments before Grace had arrived, he'd asked Ray for a sign he was listening. Maybe sending his mom had been his way of letting Chris know he was here.

"As to why you can't tell Kelly how you feel, I don't have an answer for why, not that you asked. I will tell you that if you can't give her what she needs, then you should let her go."

Her advice echoed Ray's from his dream.

"What do you think she needs?" he asked.

"Why don't you ask *her*?"

Chris nodded and leaned over to kiss her brown cheek. "Thanks, Mrs. Jackson. It was good to see you."

"You too, Chris. Don't be a stranger."

"I won't."

Chris walked back to his truck and paused on the driver's side, watching Grace over the hood of his truck. She knelt beside her son's grave, her head bent. Whether it was grief or prayer, Chris couldn't tell, but he stared as a surprising summer breeze swung her long hair to the side, and ruffled her sunshine-yellow dress.

Chris climbed inside his truck and left the cemetery. He took a turn down Main and headed to the Pocket Full of Posies Flower Shop in the heart of Sweetheart. When he walked through the door, he heard a man and a woman arguing in the back, their voices so loud they were echoing.

"Get out of my shop, Charlie Kent, before I castrate you with whatever's handy!"

That was Kenzie Olsen. She'd been two years ahead of him in school and had always been loud.

"All I said was that your roses were overpriced!" That had to be Charlie Kent, Dustin's older brother. The two of them had been lovers once upon a time, but apparently, they were mortal enemies now.

There was a loud bang and the shattering sound of broken glass.

Charlie came running through the hallway behind the counter, coming to a halt when he saw Chris.

"Hey, Chris. Didn't hear you come in. Fair warning, she's in a bit of a mood—"

"I am going to kill you, Charlie!" Kenzie yelled, coming up behind him with a vase in her hand.

"Good to see you, Chris." Charlie sped up to the door and turned to Kenzie with a grin. "See you later, Kenz."

He ducked out of the door before she could throw the other vase, which she set down on the counter with a deep exhale.

Kenzie pushed some blond tendrils that had escaped her bandana out of her red face. "That man drives me crazy."

"I can see that," Chris deadpanned.

"Sorry about the drama. What can I get you?"

Chris pointed to an assorted arrangement of bright Gerbera daisies in a mix of orange, yellow, and pink in the case behind her. "I want those."

Kenzie smiled. "Excellent. Do you want a card?"

"No, I'll be delivering these personally."

Kenzie pulled the arrangement out of the case and set them in front of him with a wink. When she handed him the price tag, he knew why. Yowza. He was in the wrong business.

"You want to make a comment about my flower prices too?" she teased.

"No, ma'am," he said, handing her his credit card.

As he was walking out, his phone rang. It was his mother, whom he adored, but balancing the vase and his phone proved tricky. He couldn't answer for at least four rings, barely managing to hit talk before it went to voicemail.

"Hey Mom, can I call you back?"

"I just wanted to let you know that we booked your ticket for Leah and Tim's vow renewal in three weeks."

Chris wrapped a sweatshirt he had in his car around the flowers to keep them from moving, then realized who his mom was talking about. "Kelly's parents?"

"Yes. Now, they're doing it in Hawaii, and I've already talked to your receptionist about clearing your schedule, so you're all set."

Except that things were incredibly confusing and tense right now, but his mother didn't need to know that. "I need to talk to Kelly first, before I confirm—"

"Kelly's fine with it, I already spoke to Leah this morning. It's all taken care of and non-refundable, so I don't want to hear anything about you being too busy. Like you always say when I ask you to come to dinner."

Forty-five seconds in before the guilt trip. Must be a new record. "Mom, please don't start. You know I've been trying to get new clients, and things are crazy right now."

"Fine, I will let it go for now. But, we will see you in Hawaii if not before. And tell Kelly she is welcome to come with you to dinner anytime. We miss her!"

Chris climbed into the driver seat and started the car. "Thanks, I will. And thanks for letting me know."

"All right, bye. Come to dinner soon, or I'll make your father call."

That was all he needed. An awkward conversation with his dad about why he was disappointing his mother.

"Okay, I will, Mom. Love you. Bye."

Chris headed for Something Borrowed's office, holding onto the flowers with one hand and the steering wheel with the other. He parked right next to Kelly's car and jumped out of his truck, whistling the whole way up to the front door.

He smiled at the receptionist as he came through, and stopped in front of Maggie St. Clair's desk. "Hey, is Kelly in?"

Maggie's frizzy brown air swung around her head, her brown eyes wide. "She is, but Mr. Ryan, she's in crisis mode."

"She's always in crisis mode."

"Mr. Ryan, I'm serious!" Maggie cried, but he ignored her.

Chris headed down the hallway and opened Kelly's office door. Inside, Kelly, Veronica, and Rylie were watching the tablet in Veronica's hand in horror.

Kelly looked up and met his gaze. Her face was deathly pale, and the bottom of his stomach dropped out.

"What happened?" he asked

"Several media outlets scooped the Valdez wedding," Rylie answered.

Chris knew how important discretion was to Kelly, but this wasn't the first time some friend of a friend had blabbed to the press. Chris came around the desk and set the vase of flowers on the flat, mahogany surface. "I'm sorry, Kel, but this has happened before. We'll just hire more security for the actual event."

"You don't understand. They said their source is someone inside Something Borrowed Wedding Solutions. Our whole reputation is built on our confidentiality and someone has trashed it."

Kelly looked so lost as she spoke, and all he wanted to do was pull her against him and hold her.

"Veronica, can you and Rylie clear the room while I talk to Kelly?"

Once the door was shut behind them, he came around the desk and did just that. Their conversation about love could wait; she needed her friend and partner right now.

"I am going to fix this." He ran his hand over her hair and down her back. "You understand? That is what I am here for."

Her arms tightened around his waist and he pushed aside the flash of awareness at the press of her breasts. "I'm scared, Chris. Everything I have worked for, my whole life...I could lose everything."

"No, you won't. I won't let that happen." He pulled away from Kelly and stroked her cheek. "And you'll always have me."

"Thank you." She wiped at her eyes, and sniffed, reaching around him for a box of tissues on her desk. "What is the first step?"

"I'll hire a guy I know to find out who really dropped a dime to the press. Just give me a few days to handle this, all right? Don't do anything. Be vague, damage control only. Just tell people that call you are looking into the allegations, but to rest assured that Something Borrowed holds its clients' privacy in the highest regard."

Kelly snorted. "If they'll believe me."

"It doesn't matter if they do or don't. You do that, and I'll handle the rest."

"I know." She patted his chest with a smile. "That's what I pay you the big bucks for, right?"

"Yep. So, try not to stress. I'll get this handled in no time."

"I am really glad I have you in my corner, Chris. I am honestly freaking out." He ran his hand up her arm and squeezed her shoulder. "It will be okay."

"What are the flowers for?" she asked abruptly.

*All right, I guess we are going to talk about it.* "I bought them for you. You said something really important and I screwed up."

"What are you talking about?" she asked.

Now, his heart fluttered nervously. "You said you loved me, and I didn't realize it wasn't our usual banter."

She seemed confused. "Yes, it was."

"It was?"

"Uh huh. Did you think I was serious?"

"Yeah. I was afraid I'd messed up again. I mean, you took off before I woke up and I thought maybe you were pissed at me."

"No, we're good. I swear. Just find out who did this."

Chris wasn't sure what to say. He'd been so sure that she'd meant it.

"Okay, I'll go make some calls. Just don't stress. Everything is going to be all right."

# Chapter 28

Everything was not all right.

It was Monday morning, and Kelly and the rest of the Something Borrowed staff had been fielding phone calls all weekend, including a very angry one from Teresa Valdez on Friday night.

"*I came to you because I was told you could be trusted and then someone in your company sold me out!*"

Kelly had tried to be calm and reassuring, but the truth was, she was a nervous wreck. She had no proof that someone outside had done this and without it, she couldn't argue or protest convincingly.

Still, she'd tried.

"It wasn't anyone at Something Borrowed, Ms. Valdez, I can promise you that."

"*Well, someone told them, and they knew intimate details about everything, including the song for my first dance! Things only Veronica and you knew. So, either it was one of you, or someone else inside your establishment went through my file. Either way, I want a full refund and I'll be postponing my wedding. It doesn't matter now that my family isn't even speaking to me!*"

Kelly was heartbroken for her, and tried to convey as such.

"I am so very sorry for everything you are going through. Rest assured, I've hired a private investigator to find out who it was and my lawyer, Mr. Ryan, is personally looking into everything."

Teresa had hung up on her, and Kelly couldn't really blame her. She'd built this company on the understanding that all private details about clients' lives and weddings would stay that way. The fact that someone had violated that agreement had brought the entire company under scrutiny.

They'd come in this morning to ten cancellation messages on the machine, with the threat that Something Borrowed would soon be contacted by their lawyers. By ten in the morning, a headache had formed in her forehead and she was ready to go home, turn off her cell, and go back to bed.

The intercom buzzed.

"Ms. Barrow, Hank Townsend is here to see you."

Kelly sank into her chair with a groan. If Hank thought that there was a leak at Something Borrowed, he'd pull his check advance and find someone else to handle his sister's wedding. It was their biggest account this season next to the Valdez wedding. She really couldn't afford to lose it.

There was a knock on her door and she called out, "Come in."

Hank smiled as he poked his head in. "Good morning. Seems you're having a busy Monday."

*Had he really not heard what happened?* He seemed completely at ease in his black T-shirt and distressed jeans, and his expression was his usual friendly façade.

"Yeah, you can call it that." She got up and came around the edge of the desk. "Hank, I just want to assure you that no one at Something Borrowed leaked details about the Valdez wedding. I have no idea what happened, but someone is ripping my company's reputation to shreds and the media thinks we sold out a client. That isn't the case and we are trying to fix it—"

He held up his hand, stopping any further defense from her. "Kelly, I know that your company is on the up and up or I never would have trusted you to handle my sister's wedding. I came by today to see if I can help in any way. I've already sent out a tweet that the allegations against you were complete shit."

Kelly sighed with relief and was tempted to hug the man, but she was trying to hold it together. If he patted her back or tried to comfort her, she would break down. "Thank you for that. Chris hired a private investigator to find out who really leaked the info, so we're just waiting on proof from him."

Hank sank into the chair in front of her desk. "Ah, Chris. He seems like a man who will save the day, I have no doubt. In the meantime, if you need anything, a hand to hold or a shoulder to cry on, I'm here for you."

Kelly laughed weakly. "I appreciate it."

"Good." He clapped his hands together with a Cheshire cat smile. "Now, should we get down to business? Just another month until the wedding and lots left to do."

"That would be great. And thank you, Hank, for your faith in me."

Hank's usual playful manner evaporated, and he cleared his throat. "I wanted you to know that I really was interested in getting to know you as more than my sister's wedding planner. I think you're a very special woman and Chris is a lucky man."

His sincere tone struck a chord in Kelly, and she was embarrassed now that she'd dragged him into her drama.

"Thank you," she whispered. "I'm also sorry for pulling you into my personal issues. It was very unprofessional."

"Kelly, I had already crossed that line the first time we met by flirting with you. I like to think we've become friends these last few weeks, and friends help each other out." He stood up once more and chucked her under the chin. "And now that we've made this fantastically awkward, I have in this folder Julie's choice of bridesmaid's dresses. She wanted to convey that she would love to have you as part of her bridal party, but having seen the dresses, I must advise that you *run*."

Kelly chuckled and reached for the folder. She had stopped being a part of weddings years ago, but with her company hanging on a tight rope, she couldn't afford to alienate the few friends she had left.

"Tell Julie I would love to be in her wedding."

"You better look at the dress before you agree. It's hashtag hideous, as the kids are saying these days."

Kelly opened the folder, her eyes traveling over the very orange ruffled dress and laughed.

"I'm in. Maybe I can convince her to go with something in periwinkle."

"That's blue, right?" Hank asked.

"Yes."

"I like blue better than orange, but we'll come back to that. Check out these flower bouquets she sent me."

Kelly stood up and glanced down at the photographs he laid out of bouquets, center pieces, and boutonnieres. All of them had painted roses in an array of colors that would have made a rainbow jealous.

"Your sister's a bit of a unicorn, isn't she?"

"You mean she likes bright colors and is unique? Yes, she is."

As they smiled at each other, Kelly covered his hand with hers. "Thank you for being my friend, Hank."

Hank stayed for an hour, going through the rest of the binder until they had a plan. After he left, Kelly sat down at her desk and let the dam of tears loose. She needed the release and let herself go for several moments until they began to slow.

Calm once more, she wiped at her eyes with Kleenex. When her vision was clear, she spotted the flowers Chris had brought her. His apology flowers.

She hadn't meant to lie about her *I love you*, but on top of everything else, she hadn't wanted to scare him away with unnecessary pressure. She needed him right now. Not just professionally, but as her friend and her lover.

Chris had stayed with her over the weekend until Saturday night, bringing little Fungi, who was completely cured and starting to grow his hair back. When his guy from LA had called, Chris had asked her to watch his kitten while he went to help his PI. Kelly had been on pins and needles waiting on a phone call or text from him, giving her any kind of update. Besides the check-ins and *I miss you* texts, though, she had heard very little from him.

Which made her think that things were not going well.

Her cell phone rang, and she came around the desk to answer. The screen flashed with Chris's smiling face holding Fungi, and she hurried to slide her thumb across the screen.

"Hey."

"Hey, sweetheart."

"How are you? Did you find out anything?"

"Yeah, we did."

Knee weakening relief rushed through her and she sank into her office chair. "You have no idea how good that is to hear. Are you going to tell me who it was?"

"Not yet. I need you to do me a favor first."

"Anything."

"Call Teresa Valdez and her fiancée and ask them to come down to your office tomorrow afternoon."

Kelly worried her bottom lip. "What if I can't get them here? As far as I know, they left town. They aren't even talking to Veronica."

"Tell them it's important. That you have the truth about who really sold the details about their wedding. That will strike their interest."

"And do we know who did it?"

"Yeah we do. You're going to be so glad to see me after you hear what I found out."

Her heart fluttered as she admitted, "I'll be glad to see you just because."

"That's really good to hear."

"Can't you tell me now, though?" She heard him chuckled and continued, "I have been a wreck for days and something concrete to tell clients would really make me feel better."

"Nope. The shock value will be better if you hear it when everyone else does."

"You're torturing me."

"I'll make it up to you, I promise."

"All right." She couldn't force him to tell her and as impatient as she was, she trusted Chris when it came to business. "When are you coming home?"

"I'm on my way to the airport now. I'll text you when I get into Sacramento."

"Be safe." *I love you.*

"I miss you, Kel."

"I miss you, too."

"See you tonight."

The call ended and Kelly set it down on the desk. Chris wouldn't ask her to reach out to Teresa if he didn't have proof Something Borrowed wasn't involved, so that took a little of the stress off her shoulders.

But there was the matter of waiting on Chris's feelings to catch up to hers.

*Relax. One problem at a time. After tomorrow, I can go back to worrying about whether Chris will ever love me the way I love him.*

# Chapter 29

Chris pulled into Kelly's driveway seven hours later. He'd spent the whole time at the airport and on the plane completely wrung out and barely able to keep his eyes open. Yet the moment he got in his car and knew that he was only an hour away from being with Kelly, he'd been reenergized.

He grabbed his carry-on from the back seat and when his foot touched the first step of the porch, the door opened, and Kelly flew outside. Her hair was thrown up in a messy bun and she wore a pair of yoga pants and a tank top, and she brought a whole new meaning to sight for sore eyes.

He barely had time to drop the bag before she threw herself into his arms.

"I have been a complete wreck without you."

Although he hated that she'd been so stressed out, it was good to hear that she needed him.

"I'm sorry, but I had to go. And now, we have everything we need to clear up Something Borrowed's reputation."

She pulled back and grabbed his hand. "Come inside and tell me everything about your trip."

Chris tugged her back to him and kissed her, adrenaline shooting through him. They hadn't kissed since before this whole mess, but he couldn't stop himself. Being away from her had been hard, especially since he knew she was struggling with worry over losing everything she'd worked for.

She sank against him, and they stood together, losing their stress and worry in the taste and feel of the other. Watching Kelly try to be strong as her life fell apart had made him furious, and he'd wanted to punish the bastard who had hurt her. It had been a gut-wrenching reaction and then when he'd had to leave her…

The only thing good about his time away from her is that he'd thought about what he needed to do to. He loved Kelly, and she deserved everything he had to give. Even if things didn't work out, if it all got messy, he wasn't going to play it scared anymore.

Kelly broke the kiss, pulling away with a smile.

"Well that was wonderfully unexpected."

"Why?"

"Because you haven't kissed me since before this all happened."

"I figured you had enough going on without me mauling you."

She shook her head. "When you kiss me, I forget everything else except how good it feels to be with you. Just now, when you pulled me to you, is the most relaxed I've been since Thursday."

He bent down and picked up his bag. "Then let's go inside and maybe I can relax you some more."

She laughed and shut the door behind him once they were inside. Fungi was curled up on the couch, practically sprawled on top of Pepper, who was grooming the kitten lovingly with his tongue.

"When did that happen?" he asked.

"Yesterday. Since the veterinarian gave Fungi a clean bill of health on Saturday, I figured he should get to know his cousin. I actually thought Pepper was going to hate his guts, but it's just the opposite. I think he loves the tiny monster more than he loves me."

Chris set his bag down with a chuckle. "I find that hard to believe."

"You're right. I am the controller of the food after all. I will always be numero uno." She walked into the kitchen and he followed behind, his gaze traveling down to her tight yoga pants hugging her backside. "Are you hungry at all?"

His eyes snapped up when he realized that she'd caught him staring at her ass and smiled sheepishly. "No, I'm fine. I grabbed something in Folsom."

She turned around with her back to the counter, her arms crossed over her chest. "Please tell me what you found. I can't stand it."

He knew she wasn't going to accept not knowing the details beforehand, but he needed her to. There was no way she wouldn't let something slip if she knew and he didn't want to risk not having the leak right where he wanted them. "It's complicated, baby. I just need you to trust me. Did you get Alejandro and Teresa to come?"

"Yeah. Turns out they hadn't left town. They'll be by at ten."

"Good."

"Are you sure you can't just tell me? I'm going to go crazy all night wondering."

Chris closed the distance between them and pulled her against him. She kept her arms crossed like a wall between them and he could understand her irritation with him, but he needed to do this. Kelly was a professional, but she would often take things personally, and if she knew who it was who had almost destroyed her, she might blow the whole thing.

"I can't tell you about who set you up, but I do need to tell you something else."

She dropped her arms and looked up at him. "All right."

"I've been stressed about what being with you will mean, and I've been a little scared. You know me. I like order; but when I'm with you, I'm a mess of emotions."

"A little insulted, but okay," she said.

"What I'm trying to tell you is that I didn't want things to change because all of my relationships had fizzled out, and I was afraid we'd be the same way. And I can't not have you in my life."

"Chris, I—"

He held up a finger. "Please, let me finish." She nodded her head. "You helped me realize that the best way to keep you in my life is to take stock of my feelings and what I want. And I want you with me, always, as my everything. It's what you've always been for me, Kelly. It just took me awhile to realize it."

He paused, taking a deep breath.

"I love you."

Kelly's full lips split into a wide grin. "I know."

Chris frowned. "No, I really love you."

"And I really know."

"Are you messing with me?" he asked.

"A little." She wrapped her arms around his waist. "Chris, I love you too. I couldn't imagine feeling the way I do about you and you not loving me too. It just didn't seem possible. So, I decided that I would take back my *I love you* and let you have this first. You know, since I've initiated everything else."

He kissed her, stroking her back with his hands. "Thank you."

"You're welcome. Now, will you take me upstairs and distract me? Otherwise, I might go crazy and torture you until you tell me what you know."

"Patience, my love," he said. "Good things come to those who wait."

"I know."

Her soft gaze warmed his heart and he picked her up, carrying her up the stairs to bed.

# Chapter 30

Kelly sat behind her desk, with Chris at her back like always. Veronica stood off to their left, while Teresa and Alejandro occupied the chairs across from them. Kelly tried hard to keep her feet from nervously dancing beneath her desk. No matter what she'd said or done, Chris wouldn't share his master plan and now that the moment of truth was there, she was seriously anxious.

She glanced behind her at Chris and he nodded.

"Since everyone is here, we can get started," Kelly said. She waved behind her at Chris. "Mr. Ryan is the company attorney, as you remember, and he has some information he'd like to share."

"Enough with the theatrics," Teresa said. "I get enough drama on my show. You said that you knew who really sold us out, so tell us."

Chris picked up the manila envelope off the desk and pulled out the papers inside. He set down a sheet of paper in front of Teresa.

"This is a copy of the check that *The Daily Gossip* wrote for the scoop on your wedding and pregnancy. Can you read the name aloud for us?"

"Juan Rodriguez. Who is that?" Teresa asked.

"That is your fiancée's legal name. Apparently, he felt Alejandro Garcia was a better name for business." Chris pulled out several more papers and Kelly leaned over to see what they were. "In case you don't believe me, this is his driver's license before he legally changed his name."

Teresa stared at it, and then turned to Alejandro. To Kelly's shock, the calm, professional Teresa flew at her fiancée, beating him over the head with her fists.

"You stupid bastard! Why would you do this? I thought you loved me!"

He grabbed a hold of her wrists and glared at her. He threw her hands away from him and snapped, "Loved you? How could you think I would love *you*? You thought you were better than me, treated me like your lap dog."

"What? Are you crazy? I wanted to *marry* you! I am having your child."

"So, *you* say," Alejandro sneered.

*Oh no he didn't.*

This time, Veronica jumped in to restrain her cousin before she beat him some more. It didn't stop the string of angry curses to escape Teresa's full lips, though.

When Teresa calmed down, Chris came around the desk and patted Teresa on the shoulder. Kelly smiled as Chris laid down another document, clearly on a roll. "Your fiancée has been a busy guy. Apparently, he wasn't too happy with the prenup you made him sign. So, while he was in town last week, he also made a stop at the producer's office for your show and let him know that you were pregnant with his child and the two of you were getting married."

Teresa's face drained of color, but Chris didn't stop, just kept pushing forward.

"Now, I don't know if he thought that his relationship with you would score him a bigger part in the show or that the studio heads would be so furious that they'd fire you, but he underestimated your appeal. They decided that they would work around your pregnancy next season with a new fantastic storyline. Congratulations, by the way." Chris shot Alejandro a look filled with mock pity, clicking his tongue. "But poor Alejandro was informed that his character would get killed off because it had reached its 'natural climatic end.' I guess that's code for 'we don't employ lowlife weasels who rat out their fiancées to get ahead.'"

"Bastard," Alejandro snarled.

"Actually, my parents were married," Chris said.

"You know what, Mr. Ryan?" Kelly said thoughtfully.

"What's that, boss?"

Kelly leaned back in her chair, her expression deceptively innocent. "I think Alejandro here is one of those men who doesn't want his woman to be more successful than he is."

Chris pretended to be shocked. "You don't say."

Alejandro sat erect in his chair, his face a stiff mask of fury.

Veronica, who had been holding her cousin back, suddenly stepped around Teresa and slapped Alejandro upside the head. Very hard, by the way his neck snapped forward and then back. He swung around in his seat, and she pointed her finger at him, only an inch from his nose. "You almost made me lose my job, *pendejo*."

Alejandro let loose with a rapid burst of Spanish, and by his expression and hand gestures, Kelly was pretty sure he was telling them all to fuck themselves.

Chris waited until Alejandro was finished before he spoke directly to Teresa. "The good news, Teresa, is that Kelly is more than happy to tear up your contract with Something Borrowed, officially and without penalty, as the evidence proves Something Borrowed was not at fault for the wedding being canceled. However, because some of the vendors had nonrefundable deposits, we cannot get those back for you."

"That's fine," Teresa said, stabbing Alejandro with a dangerous glare. "When I take him to court, I'll get my money back."

"Oh, that reminds me." Chris laid a piece of paper in front of Alejandro.

Alejandro leaned forward, squinting at the paper. "What is this?"

"That is a contract. Basically, it states you are going to contact all of the media outlets you took money from and retract your statements about Something Borrowed. In exchange, Something Borrowed will not file a lawsuit against you for defamation, and we will not release these photos to the press."

"What photos?" Alejandro asked.

Chris gave him a white envelope, and when Alejandro saw what was inside, he clutched them to his chest in horror.

Kelly was dying to know what they were of, but figured she would ask Chris later.

Chris examined his cuticles like a cop with a solid case just waiting on a confession. "I have copies, in case you were wondering if you could just destroy those. You have until tomorrow afternoon or my colleague will release the photos and you will spend years and all the money you've earned, in litigation."

Alejandro took the pen Chris held out to him with a jerk and signed the paper with hard swipes. When he stood up, and started to leave, Chris called out to him.

"I have one more document for you, but it's up to Teresa on whether or not she wants you to sign it."

Alejandro paused in the doorway, but didn't remain silent. "What does that mean, she has to decide if I sign it?"

Chris pulled one more document from the envelope and held it out to Teresa. As Kelly watched Teresa read it over, a sad little smile spread across Teresa's lips.

Then, she held out the document to Chris and nodded.

Chris stood up and handed it to Alejandro. "This is a document that will terminate your parental rights to Ms. Valdez's unborn child. In exchange, she will not file a lawsuit for the breach in your confidentiality agreement."

"What confidentiality agreement?"

"It was a subsection of your prenup. Apparently, Ms. Valdez's agent didn't trust you." Chris smiled at Teresa. "Smart man."

"Actually, woman." Teresa sniffed. "She kept telling me that he was no good, but I didn't see it."

"That's not your fault. You thought you had fallen in love with a decent human being. Just because he turned out to be slime has nothing to do with you." Chris focused his attention on Alejandro, who was practically pulsating with rage. "In conclusion, you sign and you can walk away from this with a small shred of dignity and money, or fight, and lose everything."

Alejandro took the contract and signed it against the back of the door. "I never wanted a kid anyway. I was content to just sleep with her until I could move onto bigger and better things. She was the one who didn't know how to take her pill."

Chris took the contract from him. "Classy. You really are a prize. Now, you are signing away your parental rights of your own free will?"

"Yes."

"Good, you can go then."

"One sec." Kelly came around the desk and stood in front of Alejandro. "You almost destroyed my reputation and my business I've spent the last ten years building with your petty revenge. And for what? Because you were too stupid to realize you had something really good? Or that you were so greedy you couldn't just love Teresa, you wanted to own her too?"

Alejandro scoffed and attempted to turn away, but in a flash, Kelly grabbed him by his shoulders. With a loud grunt, she brought her knee up and slammed it into his groin.

Alejandro crumbled to the ground with a silent scream. Kelly turned and flashed Chris a brilliant smile.

"Hey, thanks for those kickboxing videos. I feel a lot better now."

Chris walked over to Alejandro and helped him up. As he escorted the hobbling man out of the room, he shot Kelly an exasperated look.

Once they were out of sight, Kelly turned to Veronica and Teresa. "I guess kicking his balls up into his throat was too much?"

"I'd call it just desserts," Veronica said.

Teresa stood. "I appreciate you and your attorney discovering the truth. It would have been humiliating to find out all of this from my producers when I got back to LA."

"I am sorry to say it was selfishly motivated," Kelly said. "Something Borrowed is my life. I don't know what I'd do if I lost it."

"I am glad that it did not come to that." Teresa hugged Kelly, then held her hand out to her cousin. "Do you mind if I steal my cousin today?"

Kelly recognized the grief in the other woman's eyes. Her fiancée had turned out to be a dirt bag, and she was hurting. She wanted to be surrounded by people she loved.

"Of course. You can have her for as long as you need. And it will get better."

Veronica squeezed Kelly to her. "Thank you so much for not firing me."

Kelly laughed. "It wasn't you and I knew it. But when you get back to work, we need to talk about your event load and what to do while I'm in Hawaii at my parents' vow renewal."

Veronica's jaw dropped. "You're going to let me stay a bridesmaid?"

"Consultant. And yes, I am."

Veronica practically danced out of her office with Teresa, but the door didn't even close before Chris was back, his blue eyes narrowed. He looked pissed.

"You couldn't just let it go? You had to unman him?"

She shrugged. "Seemed a small price to pay for nearly destroying the lives of three women. Think about it; I almost lost my business and reputation. Veronica thought she was going to lose her job. And Teresa not only could have lost her show, but she would have had to share her child with that douche canoe for the rest of her life. In my opinion, he got off easy."

Chris groaned loudly. "See, this is why I didn't tell you it was him beforehand. You would have shown up at his hotel room and run him off before I managed to get him to agree to our terms."

"Is he pressing charges because I gave his nards a hate tap?"

Kelly saw his lips twitch in amusement. "No."

She came around and wrapped her arms around his neck. "Then I don't see why we're still talking about this." She stood up on her tip toes and brushed his lips with hers. "Or talking at all."

"We can't have sex here," he murmured, even as his hands drifted down to cover her back side.

"Then let's go back to my house." Laughing at his shocked expression, she added, "What? I deserve a mental health day and if you didn't hear, most of my clients have bailed, so my schedule's wide open."

Chris let her go and opened the door of her office. "Well, let's get the hell out of here and see if we can find something to pass the time."

# Chapter 31

Two weeks later, Kelly stood on a sandy beach on Honolulu, her bare feet sinking into the soft sand. The wind caught the flowing skirt of her coral dress, dancing the fabric around her legs and whipping her hair out of the elegant updo and into her face. The lullaby of the ocean played under the soft classical music her mother had chosen for the pre-ceremony.

Next to her, her dad stood tall in a black tux, his silver hair thinning at the top, but his hazel eyes just as sharp as when she was a child. The sun beat down on him from above and she could see the sheen of sweat on his skin from the humidity.

"Are you nervous, Daddy?" she teased.

He snorted. It didn't take a genius to realize that her dad had only gone along with this vow renewal because her mother had insisted, and he wanted to be anywhere but standing in the humid Hawaiian air in a *penguin suit*. His words, not hers.

A handful of her extended family sat in the white folding chairs on either side of the aisle, along with her parents' closest friends. Palm trees swayed in the distance, and the looming tower of their hotel cast a shadow across the guests.

And then, in the third row back next to his parents, sat Chris, wearing a gray suit and giving her the goofiest smile. His hair was freshly cut, but the sunshine hit his locks, causing a glow atop his head, showcasing the highlights in the short strands. His blue eyes perfectly matched his tie; she knew that because she'd picked it out last week and slipped it into his suitcase.

The bridal processional started, and everyone stood.

Kelly watched as her mother came out of the sliding glass door of her parents' hotel suite and walked slowly down the stairs. As she made her way across the sand, Kelly noted the high-necked white dress that gathered under her mother's breasts and flowed down to the sand. Her mother held up the skirt of her dress with one hand and her gorgeous bridal bouquet in the other. Her dark hair framed her face in a straight A-line cut, and a wreath of white roses and baby's breath sat atop her head.

From a distance, her mother appeared younger, but as she drew nearer, Kelly could make out every line around her eyes and mouth. She'd earned them through years of smiles and tears, laughter and heartache.

In Kelly's eyes, she was the most beautiful bride she'd ever seen.

Kelly shot a glance at her dad. Her eyes grew misty at the transfixed expression on his face as he stared at her mother coming down the white fabric aisle runner. There was so much love there that Kelly was almost envious.

Then she looked at Chris again and his lips moved. After a moment, she realized he was mouthing something.

*I love you.*

Kelly wanted to say it back, but they hadn't told their parents yet. After two weeks of blissfully tearing each other's clothes off every chance they got, they'd spent the last two nights apart. It wasn't that they didn't want to tell their families, but she hadn't wanted to draw attention away from her parents' happiness and Chris had been worried his mother wouldn't be able to resist meddling if they told them too soon. They still had three days left in Hawaii; plenty of time to let the cat out of the bag.

Her mother held her hand out to her father, and before turning her back on Kelly, her mom gave her the brightest smile she'd ever seen.

The non-denominational minister her mother had hired was a robust man named Hani. He'd told them all that his mother had named him Hani, which meant happy, because she swore he came out of her laughing. It was either funny or disturbing, depending on how you looked at it.

"Family and friends," Hani said loudly. "We are here to celebrate the recommitment ceremony of Leah and Tim Barrow. Forty years ago, these two beautiful souls vowed to love, honor, and cherish each other for the rest of their lives...and in my opinion, they're well on their way to fulfilling those vows."

After reciting the same poem that they had used at their wedding, he asked them to say their vows.

Kelly watched her father sweat bullets as he spoke, telling her mother that after all these years, she wasn't the girl he married. She was even better, because the twists and turns they'd ridden together had made her a stronger version of that girl. And she was even more beautiful now because of all that she'd accomplished.

That got Kelly's eyes watering, but her mother pushed her over the edge when she told him that he was more than the man of her dreams. He was the one she knew would stick around long after the music faded and she woke up. He was the hand she always wanted to be holding before she closed her eyes at night.

Kelly pulled a tissue she had hidden in her bouquet out, and dabbed at her eyes as her parents exchanged the new, upgraded rings, sliding them onto each other's fingers. When the ceremony was finally over, Kelly slipped her arm through her Uncle Kenny's, her dad's younger brother, and they followed the happy couple back down the aisle to a secluded area of the beach for pictures. Although she smiled and posed and hugged and kissed, she couldn't wait to find Chris and be in his arms.

An hour later, Kelly snuck up behind Chris while he was getting a drink, and slipped her arms around his waist.

"Hey, handsome."

"Hi." He covered her hands on his abdomen with his own. "I missed you. Think we might be able to sneak off for a little while? I wouldn't mind getting to kiss my girlfriend."

"That could probably be arranged." She let him go and came around to face him. "Or, we could just tell our parents we're together now."

His brow furrowed. "I thought you wanted to wait so we didn't take the attention away from your parents."

"I think the two of us together would pretty much be the best vow renewal present we could get my mom."

"And your dad?" Chris asked.

Kelly shrugged. "He'll get used to it."

"That's not comforting. At all."

"Come on, sissy. Let's get this over with." Kelly laced her fingers with his and asked, "Unless you aren't ready, in which case, I will back away slowly before either of our mothers notice anything suspicious."

Chris brought her hand up to his mouth, brushing her knuckles with his lips. "Ready when you are."

Kelly's heart practically took flight out of her chest, it was fluttering so hard. Together, they made their way over to her parents, who were standing next to the buffet.

Suddenly, a strong odor of seafood filled her nostrils and her stomach turned violently.

She pulled up short as her throat constricted, bile rising up the back.

"Kel? You okay?"

She shook her head. "That smell. It's awful."

"What smell?"

"Seafood."

Chris seemed to be sniffing the air, and then studied her. "You look a little green. Want me to take you back to your room to lie down?"

"No, I'm not missing this. It was probably just something I ate. See," she said, breathing through her mouth. "All better now."

"If you're sure..."

"I am. Do you maybe want to go tell your parents first?" She didn't want to tell Chris that she was afraid if she got any closer to the buffet she was going to upchuck all over the place.

"We can do that."

Chris let her lead him over to where his parents stood. Marcy and Keith Ryan were younger than her parents by several years. While both of his parents were blond, Kelly always thought Chris looked more like his father with his mother's eyes.

"Chris. Kelly. Wasn't it a beautiful ceremony? I'm trying to convince your father we should do something like this for our anniversary. Maybe in the highlands of Scotland or something."

"I'm not going to wear a kilt," Keith said. "Your mother discovered that show *Outlander* and now all she can talk about is going to Scotland and dressing up as thought we were in the fifteen hundreds."

"What your father won't admit is that he's watched several episodes of the show and loved it. He even does a lovely Scottish accent. You should show them, darling."

Chris's dad looked murderous and Kelly laughed, squeezing Chris's hand in hers. She was surprised that Marcy hadn't noticed their entwined fingers, as they weren't doing anything to hide it.

"I want to see *Outlander*, but I don't have cable," Kelly said.

Chris groaned. "She just got through binging *Reign* a month ago. I really cannot take another romantic show so soon."

Kelly bumped him with her hip. "Stop it, you were totally Team Bash. Admit it."

"Fine, the show was okay. Bash was the only cool character though. What can I say? I love a redeemed bad boy," Chris teased.

Kelly saw Marcy's gaze finally fall on their hands and her eyes widened. "Oh, my God. Are you two...are you dating?"

Chris smiled at Kelly, making her stomach flip. "Yeah, Mom. For a couple weeks now."

"Oh! I am so happy." Marcy hugged first Chris and then pulled Kelly into a tight embrace. "I can't believe you didn't tell me! Isn't that wonderful, Keith?"

"Yes, of course." Keith was usually a little hard to read, but as he slapped his hand on his son's arm, Kelly saw the genuine affection in his eyes. "Congratulations."

"Thanks. We haven't told Kelly's parents yet, so if you could just keep this to yourselves until we talk to Leah and Tim that would be great."

"Talk to us about what?"

Kelly turned to the right to find her mom and dad standing next to them.

"Well, we wanted you to know that Chris and I are dating."

Kelly's mom squealed louder than Chris's as she embraced them both. "I knew it! The two of you have been acting shifty since you got here!"

"We have not been acting shifty," Kelly protested.

Then Kelly's mom was hugging Marcy, and Kelly turned to Chris with a bemused expression. "We told them."

"Yep. Think we can finally stay in the same hotel room?" he whispered.

Kelly glanced at her dad, who was watching them with a protective gleam in his eyes.

"Maybe we should just wait until we get home."

Chris followed her line of vision and swallowed. "Good plan."

Kelly stood up on her tiptoes and kissed his cheek. "I love you, though."

"I love you, too. Now back up a step. Your dad looks ready to throttle me."

# Chapter 32

The morning of Julia Townsend's wedding, Kelly felt like death warmed over. For the last week, she'd been tired and nauseous. The smell of cooking meat turned her stomach, especially. Chris had made sausage and eggs yesterday morning, and Kelly had about dry heaved her back out.

Kelly wanted to blame the stress of the last few weeks, but things were actually turning out better than she imagined. With Hank and Teresa's endorsement and Alejandro's retraction, most of her clients had come back with their apologies. She'd been humble and understanding, of course. In addition, they'd booked four more weddings for later in the summer and early fall. Something Borrowed was officially in the clear.

Sitting in Julia's room at the Love Shack Hotel, Kelly nibbled on some toast while Julia and her three reed-thin friends stood in front of the available mirrors. It was just before eleven, and even though the wedding wasn't taking place until four, Julia had wanted them to get there early so they had plenty of time for hair and makeup.

And as a bonus, Kelly had managed to convince Julia that her maid of honor and bridesmaids would look much better in periwinkle than pumpkin orange.

"Feeling sick?" Julia asked, her accent less defined than her brother's. She sat down next to Kelly on the bed and took a sip from the bottled water in her hand. Julia was dark haired like her brother, with unnatural green eyes. They were so bright, Kelly was convinced they might just glow in the dark. Clad in a salmon pink camisole and yoga pants, she was tall, lithe, and gorgeous.

And incredibly down to earth, just like her brother.

"Yeah, a little. The last week, actually."

Julia grabbed a Danish from the room service plate. "Oh, how far along are you?"

"Pardon?" Kelly asked.

Julia ran her hand over her flat stomach. "I'm fourteen weeks, but you can't tell, right? I'm over most of that morning sickness stuff, although certain smells can still make me queasy."

Kelly blinked several times, completely boggled by what the other woman was telling her. "Wait, I'm not pregnant."

Julia looked aghast. "Oh, sorry. I shouldn't have assumed."

Kelly's heart pounded loudly in her ears. "Does your brother know you're pregnant?"

"I told him yesterday. He was actually excited about it. I gave him a little onesie that says, 'My Uncle kicks arse.'"

Oh yeah, Hank would love that.

"Well, congratulations. I am so happy for you."

"Thank you. And sorry again about the mix up."

"It's fine."

One of her bridesmaids called her name and she patted Kelly's knee. "I appreciate everything you've done and being a part of this. My brother speaks highly of you."

When she was gone, Kelly mentally calculated the last time she'd had her period. She had never been great at remembering her pill, even when she set her alarm on her phone, but it hadn't been an issue, since she wasn't sexually active.

Until Chris.

Kelly stood up and abandoned her toast in the trash. "Do you girls need anything? Coffee? Tea?"

"Yes, that would be amaaaazing," Julia's maid of honor, Aurora, said.

After taking down their drink order, Kelly hurried down the hallway to the elevator, tapping her toe against the floor as she waited for it to open.

Finally, she managed to get out of the hotel and head over to the supermarket without anyone stopping her to chit chat. There was no way. Even with human error, the pill was like 90% effective. She just had some kind of bug, was all.

Kelly grabbed the first test she saw, and went through Jason Dalton's line. He was eighteen and barely glanced at her item as he checked her out.

She couldn't be gone too long, and so going home was out of the question. The bathroom at Something Borrowed's office would have to suffice.

Kelly shoved the test box into her purse and walked through the glass doors. Maggie shot her a look of confusion as she hurried past.

"Hey, boss, shouldn't you be getting ready for the Townsend wedding?"

"Yes, I just forgot something in my office."

She checked over her shoulder to see if Maggie was watching her, but it was clear. She ducked into the bathroom and locked the door with a click.

Three minutes and thirty seconds later, she was staring at two pink lines in the view window of the pregnancy test.

*Oh, my God, I am having Chris's baby.*

What was she going to tell him? That she was great at running a business and lousy at remembering to take her pill? That would go over well.

Kelly continued to stare at the results of the test and mixed with the fear and the anxiety was…excitement. She was *pregnant*. There was a tiny person growing inside her.

Of course, her mother would say she was doing everything ass backwards if she told her, but there was no reason to go there yet. If anyone was going to hear this news first, it was going to be Chris.

Kelly slipped the stick back into the box and then into her purse. After she washed her hands, she tried to sneak back out, but…

"Hey, boss, find what you were looking for?" Maggie asked, cheerfully.

"I did, Maggie. Thanks for asking."

Kelly made it back to the hotel with coffees in hand, and after hours of beautification, she stood along the side of the outdoor reception's dance floor, watching Julia share her first dance with her award-winning director husband. The Mason jar favors filled with mixed berry jam sat on every table with a sweet little card attached, thanking each guest for sharing in their special day. Kelly had been surprised that all three hundred guests, some of them traveling as far as Scotland, had come in. Every hotel in a fifty-mile radius had been booked to accommodate everyone.

The room sparkled with glittering ribbons of lavender, blue, yellow, green, and pink. The brightly colored rose centerpieces were arranged in white vases.

The entire affair had run smoothly and the happy couple seemed to be having the time of their lives.

"Well done."

Kelly jumped as Hank came up alongside her, standing shoulder to shoulder as they watched Julia. He wore a black tux on his top half and a blue and red kilt. The look was rather dashing, and more than a few women had been checking out his legs through the whole event.

"Thank you. Hats off to you too, since you had a hand in it."

"I suppose I did lend a hand."

Kelly glanced his way when he didn't say more and she realized that Hank looked nervous.

"Something on your mind?" she asked.

"Actually, I was wondering. Your assistant, Veronica..."

"Yeah?"

"Is she single?"

Kelly's eyes widened. "I'm sorry, but it just sounded like you were asking about my employee's relationship status. Besides, aren't you going back to La-La-Land tomorrow?"

"I was looking at buying property up here between filming and I find her...fascinating."

She laughed.

"What, you don't think I'm sincere?" he asked.

"Oh no, I think you mean it. But I also know Veronica."

"And?"

Kelly patted his shoulder. "If you screw with her, she will eat you alive."

"Does that mean I have your blessing?"

"You don't need my blessing. If you want to ask Veronica out, go for it. Just don't be surprised if she turns you down flat."

"Does she ever talk about me?"

"Besides calling you weird? No."

"That's discouraging."

Kelly glanced at her watch and relief spread through her. She stood up on her tiptoes and kissed Hank's cheek. "If anyone could win Veronica over, it's you. Now, if you'll excuse me, this woman's work is done, and I am ready for bed."

Hank gave Kelly a hug before she could pull away. "It was wonderful working with you, Ms. Barrow."

"Likewise, Mr. Townsend."

Kelly slipped away from the reception and headed to her car. The moment she was inside, she texted Chris.

*Hey, I'm done. Can I come over?*

*Yeah, I've been waiting for you.*

*See you soon.*

Kelly took a deep breath and started the car, scared to death of how he was going to react when she dropped this bomb on him.

*It's Chris. Mr. Supportive. It will be fine.*

# Chapter 33

Chris pulled the plane tickets out of his drawer, rolling them over in his hands. On the way home from Hawaii, Kelly had gone on and on about all the places she wanted to see, starting with Ireland and Scotland and working her way down to England, France, Italy, and Spain. She'd been so animated, talking about the places she'd always dreamed of going, that Chris had come home inspired. He'd been researching the best times to travel all week and impulsively bought plane tickets for them in the middle of September. It gave him two months to book hotels, plot train routes, and above all, plan how he was going to ask Kelly to be his wife.

Watching her stand up there with her parents had been the moment he'd known he wanted to take that step with Kelly. He didn't care if they had only technically been together a month; they had been the other half of a whole for a lot longer than that.

Fungi jumped up onto his bed and meowed loudly. Chris put the plane tickets back in his drawer and picked the kitten up, placing him over his shoulder.

"Sorry, was I ignoring you?"

The loud rumble of his purr echoed in Chris's ear as he headed out to the living room. Headlights brightened wall the far wall and Chris waited just inside the door for Kelly to come in.

The minute she opened the door, Chris saw it. The 'oh shit, I have something big to tell you' face.

"Hey, you okay?" he asked.

"Yeah, I just…I've got something big to tell you."

Chris took her hand and pulled her close. "Can I get a kiss first?"

Kelly's eyes sparkled a bit as she said, "Sure, if you get rid of the cat butt in my face."

Chris turned his head and chuckled. He lifted Fungi up and set him on the back of the couch. "How is that?"

"Much better."

They shared a soft, gentle kiss and when they pulled apart, Chris heard Kelly sigh shakily.

"Baby, what is it?"

She took held tight to his hand and led him over to the couch, motioning him to sit. They sat at the same time, their knees touching.

"I need you to know that I didn't plan this. I take full responsibility, but I didn't mean for it to happen."

Chris heart slammed against his breast bone in dread. "Are you…are you trying to tell me you want to be with someone else?"

"What?" Her expression warred between shock and outrage. "No! Have I given you any indication I'm not completely devoted to you?"

"I'm sorry, but your tone was so apologetic and—"

"No, no, it's not anything like that. I'm pregnant."

Chris stilled, letting her words sink in. "You're pregnant."

"Yes."

"Having my baby?"

"Uh huh."

He paused, waiting for the perfect response to come…

"Okay."

Kelly's eyebrows shot up her forehead. "I just told you something that could ultimately alter our lives forever and all you've got is okay?"

"What do you want me to say?" he asked.

"I don't know. How you feel about it?"

"I thought…I thought you were on the pill?"

"I am, but I'm not great about taking it at the same time every day, which makes it less effective. If you want to scream and get pissed at me, I completely understand."

Chris didn't know how to answer that, so he just squeezed her hands and stood. "Stay right here. I'll be back."

"Really? You have to go right now?"

"Yeah, but just give me a minute."

Chris sensed her irritation, even as he made his way down the hallway. He went into his bedroom and pulled out the airline tickets.

Chris came back down and she was walking out the door. "Hey, Kel, stop."

He caught her on the front porch and when he took her hand and pulled her around gently, he caught the shimmer of tears. "Kelly, come on, don't cry. I just wanted to show you something!"

"And you had to show me right this second?"

Chris held the plane tickets out to her. "Here."

Kelly took them reluctantly, and he knew the exact moment she realized what they were.

"Ireland."

"Yeah, to be followed by Scotland, England, France, Italy, and Spain. I have several weeks planned for us."

"But…what does that have to do with me being pregnant?"

"Not a thing. That's what I'm trying to say. I'm not mad. We were both consenting adults. I could have worn a condom if I was really worried that this could happen, but I didn't." Chris laid his hand over her stomach and looked her in the eyes. "I should be asking if you want this?"

Kelly covered his hands with hers. "I do."

"Well, I hope this isn't presumptuous, but maybe we can change this trip to a honeymoon."

Kelly shook her head. "Chris, you don't have to marry me just because I'm pregnant. This isn't the 1950s."

"I know, but you see, I got this yesterday. I just saw it and thought it looked just like you."

Chris pulled the velvet jewelry box out of his pocket and Kelly covered her mouth with her hands.

He popped the ring box open, showing off the two-carat diamond with two tourmaline stones on either side.

"I was going to save this for September, and ask you inside a castle or maybe the top of the Eiffel Tower, but honestly, why wait? I know what I want."

Chris brushed his lips over hers and whispered, "Be mine, sweetheart. I'm begging you."

Kelly threw her arms around him. "I love you."

"I know, but that's not the answer I'm looking for."

"Yes, yes!" She kissed him, and he tasted the salt of her tears on her lips.

When they finally came up for air, he slipped the ring on her finger and twined his fingers with hers.

"Just one thing. Do you think you can plan a wedding in two months?"

Kelly gave him one of her sassiest looks. "Excuse me? Don't you know who you're talking to?"

Chris laughed and pulled her into his arms on the couch. As they snuggled in, Chris drifted off to sleep, Kelly's warm breath fanning the side of his neck.

Chris climbed up stone stairs surrounded by green rolling hills. He knew he needed to get to the top, even if he wasn't sure why yet.

When he finally made it, he stared out over a deep stone cliff and the white capped waves of the ocean rolling up onto the beach.

"Beautiful, isn't it?"

Chris wasn't even surprised by Ray's presence, but he was a little shocked to find his friend wearing a kilt and holding a bag pipe under his arm.

"What are you doing?"

"Hey, it's not my fault your twisted mind insists on dressing me up."

"I am so sorry," Chris said.

"Naw, it's cool. I got awesome legs for this." Ray leveled him with a dark, serious gaze. "So, you and Kelly are getting married?"

"Yeah."

"And having a baby."

"Looks like."

"Congratulations. I'm glad you finally worked your shit out."

Ray started to walk past him for the stairs and Chris grabbed his arm. "Hey, where are you going?"

Ray patted his cheek. "My work here is done, bud. I can finally sit around all day playing the..." Ray looked down at the instrument in his hand and shrugged. "Whatever the hell this is and floating around on clouds."

"Are you going to be okay?"

"Probably bored, but it's better than the alternative."

"Is there anything I can do?" Chris asked.

"Actually, there is one thing..."

Chris woke up with a start, sucking in air. Kelly lifted her head off his chest with a sleepy frown.

"Hey, you okay?"

"Yeah, just a dream."

"Wanna talk about it?" she mumbled.

He kissed the top of her head and held her close. "Someday, I'll tell you all about it."

# Epilogue

Inside the brightly lit hospital room, full of bustling nurses and interns, a miracle was about to happen.

"Oh, my God, what fresh hell is this?!" Kelly Ryan screamed, squeezing her husband's hand as hard as she could.

Chris stood beside her hospital bed, looking rumpled and pale. He winced, and she felt him try to extract his hand from hers. "Ow, ow, babe, babe, my fingers are starting to crack!"

"So is my pelvis!"

Kelly thought she heard a snort and focused on Chris's face with narrowed eyes. "Did you just laugh?"

"No," he said with a completely straight face.

"I am in labor with your unborn child and you're laughing at my pain?" His mouth twitched with mirth, even as he lied. "Honey, I'm not, I swear!"

The pain subsided slightly, and Kelly flopped back against the hospital mattress, her muscles aching. Her contractions had started six hours ago and had been barely a twinge at the time. So, of course she'd told the doctor she didn't need an epidural. She was tough.

Now, with violent viselike pain hitting her every minute, she was over this.

"Okay, Kelly, I want you to bear down on the next contraction," the doctor said through his facemask. His tone was calm and soothing, and she was tempted to lift her foot up and kick him.

"You hear that, babe? After this next one, he'll be out, and the pain will be gone."

Her husband's jovial words did nothing to alleviate her dark thoughts; now she was imagining pinching him.

"Chris..." the doctor said, warningly. The man probably didn't want Chris getting her hopes up in case he was wrong.

*God, I hope he's right. How can women do this for twenty hours?!*

The pain built once more and Kelly planted her feet on the hospital bed. Holding tight to Chris's hand once more, she pushed, her mouth opening wide as she released a cry that would have sent a chill down Dracula's spine.

"Great job, Kelly. We're almost there. I can see the baby's head. Just one more hard push and we'll be done."

Even with the doctor's reassurance, Kelly still wasn't convinced. Her whole body ached and sweat covered her skin like a layer of slime. She was bone tired and wished she could just curl up into a ball.

"I don't know if I can," she whispered.

Chris held her hand tight until she met his gaze. "Yes, you can," Chris said firmly. "You remember on our honeymoon, when I rolled down that hill in Scotland and sprained my ankle?" Chris smiled tenderly, his blue eyes far away as he reminded her, "You carried me on your back all the way to where the bus was parked. You are the strongest woman I know."

Kelly wanted to laugh and cry at the same time. "I never realized you were so heavy until I had to give you a piggyback ride."

He leaned over and kissed her forehead, his voice soft and low. "I want you to think of that, the feeling of pushing through the pain. I know this is hard, but I am right here with you. I love you."

Kelly took several deep breaths and as the pain climbed again, she hollered, "I know!"

Kelly's eyes filled with tears as pain ripped through her followed by the heavenly wash of relief.

And then the sweetest sound in the world filled the room.

"Congratulations, mama, you did it," the doctor said.

The high-pitched wail that had alerted her to her child's birth subsided, and she lifted her head, her gaze following the nurse hungrily as she carried the child around to their side.

"Would you like to cut the cord, daddy?"

Kelly met Chris's tear-filled blue eyes. "Yes, I would."

While Chris separated her from their child, she laughed breathlessly. "I did it."

Chris smiled tenderly at her as the nurse took the baby across the room. "Yeah, you did." He picked up a washcloth from the side table by her bed and wiped her sweaty brow. "I am so proud of you."

"Are you ready to meet your son?" the nurse asked, holding out a blanket-wrapped bundle to Kelly.

Kelly and Chris had agreed to be surprised, choosing a name for a girl and a name for a boy just in case. As the nurse placed the baby in Kelly's arms, Chris wrapped his own around both Kelly and their boy.

"We have a son," Kelly whispered.

"Hey, guy." Chris kissed her temple. "He's perfect."

"Do you have a name yet?" the doctor asked.

Kelly thought back to that cool December night. It was almost Christmas and they were just decorating the tree when the baby kicked her. She'd grabbed Chris's hand and put it over her stomach, right as a hard jab had pushed against her skin.

*"He's a fighter,"* Chris said.

*"Yeah, he is."*

To her surprise, Chris had stopped stroking her abdomen and told her about his dreams of Ray. That he'd had them infrequently after he'd died, but just before they got together he was having them every time they were intimate. He told her about the last one, how they stood inside a castle, looking out over the ocean. At first, Kelly had laughed, never imagining Ray in a kilt.

And then Chris said, *"He made one last request. He suggested we tell our child all about their Uncle Ray."*

Kelly wasn't sure if she had really believed it was Ray visiting him, but she'd taken Chris's hand and squeezed. *"I've got a better idea."*

Now, Kelly kissed Chris sweetly before she answered. "His name is Raymond. Raymond Christian Ryan."

# Acknowledgments

This book would not have been possible without my understanding husband and amazing kids. I love you. To my awesome agent, Sarah, who listens when I need to talk and is always rooting for me. Thank you for being on my side. For my fantastic editor, Norma, who makes my books better and believed in this series. Thank you. To my friend, Tina Klinesmith, who is my sister from another mister. Thank you for every mind meld and two-hour phone conversation. Thanks to my parents, my in-laws, siblings, aunts and friends. Your love and support make this journey possible. To the amazing women who make up my Rockers. I love your guts. And to all the readers who have followed me over the years. Thank you for reading.

# Meet the Author

An obsessive bookworm, **Codi Gary** likes to write sexy small-town contemporary romances with humor, grand gestures, and blush-worthy moments. When she's not writing, she can be found reading her favorite authors, squealing over her must-watch shows, and playing with her children. She lives in Idaho with her family.

Visit her on the web at www.codigarysbooks.com.

# Don't Call Me Sweetheart

*Weddings are big business in picturesque Sweetheart, California, and Something Borrowed's rent-a-bridesmaid service is thriving among the Hollywood elite. For the women who work there, a walk down the aisle is just a paycheck—until the right guy makes it priceless . . .*

**RULE #1: GROOMSMEN ARE STRICTLY OFF LIMITS**

Marley Stevenson never imagined her stint as a rented Maid of Honor would practically become a career. Then again, nothing in her life has gone according to plan. At least the money's good—and she needs it to pay off student loans and help out her mom. But the job has rules, which have never been an issue . . . until one encounter with a gorgeous best man—and his swoon-worthy Southern accent—sends Marley reeling.

Determined to get through the weekend with her professional reputation intact, Marley grits her teeth and sends out her best "unavailable" vibes, but Luke Jessup doesn't give up that easy. A former Marine and a current SWAT team officer, his focus is legendary—and it's on Marley. Jeopardizing her job is bad enough, and starting a relationship based on half-truths is worse—yet Marley is beginning to wonder if certain risks are worth taking, especially in the name of true love . . .

# Kiss Me, Sweetheart

*The bridesmaids and groomsmen for hire at Sweetheart, California's Something Borrowed have the cure for celebrity wedding headaches. But even a job that's strictly business can lead to the real thing . . .*

**RULE #2: DON'T UPSTAGE THE BRIDE AND GROOM**

Rylie Templeton had big dreams, until she quit culinary school to take care of her father and signed on with Something Borrowed. Suddenly years have gone by and she's still a bridesmaid-for-hire, with her idea to open a gourmet bakery on the back burner. Scoring a high-profile wedding could help turn her life around, if only she didn't have to share the spotlight with her coworker, the insufferable—and undeniably gorgeous—Dustin Kent.

Instructed to make it work, Rylie plunges into the wedding festivities with Dustin by her side. If only she could convince him to turn his spectacular charm on someone else! But the enigmatic, reformed playboy has his own ideas about romance, and they all include Rylie. As the nuptials get closer, Rylie realizes that Dustin's wooing is actually working, and that the two of them might make a good team in more ways than one . . .